Chosen by Random

Richard Green

ISBN: 978-0-9930695-2-9

Copyright © 2018 Richard Green

The right of Richard Green to be identified as the author of this work has been asserted in accordance with the Copyright, Designs and Patents act 1988. All rights reserved. This book is sold subject to the condition that it shall not, by way of trade or otherwise, be lent, resold, hired out, or otherwise circulated without the publisher's prior consent in any form of binding or cover other than that in which it is published and without a similar condition, including this condition being imposed on the subsequent purchaser

Set in Georgia

Published by
Bardic Media, Unit 601,
10 Southgate Road,
London N1 3LY

I would like to thank Random,
whoever they are, for choosing these pieces.
I suspect they may be a number.

Table of Contents

I'm Sorry I Haven't a Clue	- 7
Samantha Amazing	- 8
Another Convincing Performance	- 9
Memorandum	- 14
Art for Art's Sake	- 16
The Girl on the Train	- 20
A Cup of Coffee with Anne Boleyn	- 21
The Answering Machine	- 24
The Lion Tamer	- 27
The Astronomer (Part One)	- 28
The Balloon	- 32
Lucky for Some	- 33
Armour of a Fool	- 37
Sergeant Leopard	- 42
Dialogue between Two Lords of Creation	- 46
Cool it Dad	- 47
Morning Routine	- 49
The Fish Market	- 50
Conversation Piece	- 51
The Astronomer (Part Two)	- 54
Slave Labour	- 60
St George	- 61
Before The Fall	- 63
Merton and Callum	- 64
Midnight Train	- 65
Night Patrol	- 72
The Door	- 74
Picture This	- 75
The Watcher on the Shore	- 81
The Unhappy Prince	- 82
The Boat	- 84
Burglar Bill's Nasty Experience	- 90
Eeyore's Cathedral	- 92
Dr Gilchrist's Eventful Morning	- 93
Eurostar Adventure	- 95
An Unforeseen Delay	- 98
The Writer	- 99

I'm Sorry, I Haven't a Clue

I was relaxing in my favourite armchair when the doorbell rang. Standing on the step was a tallish, rather mournful-looking, middle-aged gent with slicked-back hair and a drooping moustache.

"Inspector Hound, CID," he said showing me a warrant card which looked suspiciously home-made. "Did you realise there was a dead body in your wheelie-bin? I have a description. 'Woman aged about sixty-five, medium height, slightly built, grey hair, tortoiseshell glasses, wearing a floral dress and beige cardigan'."

"That sounds like my wife," I said.

I wasn't being completely honest. True, Emily and I DID have a row. Emily was going on about the same old thing again. She was always nagging me about my habit of shooting all the tabby cats in the area with my Elephant Gun. She said we were becoming social outcasts and that she was a laughing stock at the Bridge Club. I pointed out that if you didn't get them early – shoot them while they were still cats, they grew up into tigers and where would we be then eh?

Anyway, the sight of her talking to her damn plants in the conservatory caused something to snap inside me. I took the heavy brass candlestick I just happened to be holding, gave a good overarm swing (I used to open the bowling for the regiment when I was in Poona) and brought it down hard on the back of Emily's head.

What to do with the body? Bit of a problem. Suddenly I had a brainwave! The professor-chappie who lived over the road was obsessively neat and fastidious. I reckoned if I dumped Emily in HIS lounge, he wouldn't just hoover round her body, like most normal people, but would be sure to tidy her up and put her in his wheelie-bin.

"I hope you don't think I had anything to do with my wife's death," I said.

"Oh no, sir. It was that professor-bloke. His fingerprints were all over the body. We've got him bang to rights."

I used gloves to move the body but, as I guessed – the absent-minded professor hadn't. One thing DID trouble me, though. Why did he dump Emily in MY bin? Of course! What was his subject? LOGIC! She was MY wife so logically she should be in MY bin.

I had taken out an insurance policy on Emily's life a couple of weeks ago so I was going to come in for a tidy sum. A blonde bit of stuff from down the street had been giving me the eye lately. Might try my luck there.

"Have you found the murder weapon?" I asked.

"Yes sir. A piece of lead piping. It was hidden under a cushion in the sofa in the professor's lounge."

I knew that. I had placed it there.

"There is one more thing, Colonel Mustard. Leaving dead bodies in wheelie bins is against the law. And as your wife's body WAS found in your bin, you ARE liable."

Then the blighter gave me a ticket for eighty quid and I had to stump up. All in all, though, not a bad result. True I was eighty quid down but then I HAD got away with murder. Amazing how bad the rozzers are at this game. Bad luck on Professor Plum, of course. Now, where did I put that Viagra?

Samantha Amazing

The crowd gasped in horror as, high above their heads, Samantha Amazing slipped from the strong hands gripping her wrists. Then, at the last moment, Samantha saved herself, grabbing the trapeze that, miraculously, swung towards her. The audience burst into wild applause.

Tall and athletic, Samantha had trained as a dancer. When a rebellious teenager, she really had run away to join the circus.

One night, Samantha Amazing missed the trapeze, crashed to the ground and lay very still. She had broken her back and was confined to a wheelchair for the rest of her life. Aged twenty-four, she would never walk again.

Soon afterwards, Samantha began having a dream. Always the same dream. She was running barefoot along a golden beach, in a flowing white dress, her long hair streaming behind her. She could hear the crashing surf. She could feel the sun hot on her face and the warm sand trickling between her toes.

Samantha went to a psychiatrist to help her 'manage her condition'. She was fascinated to discover that the psychiatrist actually kept a collection of shrunken heads in a glass cabinet. She had thought that was a myth.

He seemed a kind man, so, to please him, she told him 'all about herself'.

"Remember one thing, Samantha," he said. "You may feel imprisoned in a wheelchair, unable to move. In your dream, though, you are always free."

But in her dream, Samantha was never free.

Because she knew it was a dream.

Another Convincing Performance

Now he was clear of the London traffic, Henry Vulture eased the Jag up to eighty. Henry was a property tycoon. Puffy-faced and overweight after decades of lavish living, he didn't look in the least like a vulture – rather he resembled a stuffed goose. Henry had a new development project in mind and was driving down to Dorset to view the proposed location. Of course his minions had already conducted a thorough survey but Henry always liked to see the area for himself before he made a final decision, which is why he had forsaken the chauffeur-driven Rolls and was now hurtling along the M3.

A couple of hours later he arrived at his destination. He parked the car and got out to inspect the scene: a straggle of cottages and small houses, a church, a general stores, a pub – in short, a typical English village. Perfect for his scheme. It would all have to be knocked down.

In his mind's eye Henry could see a wonderful vision of the future: the stylish executive homes, the Michelin-starred restaurant, a high-class country club, a fashionable casino. And, yes, why not? A purpose-built marina.

Admittedly, there was no vast expanse of water nearby but mechanical diggers could be hired couldn't they? Henry was now becoming really excited. Just think of it! The architect-designed lakeside villas, the exclusive yacht club, an up-market health spa. The opportunities for making really serious money were endless.

Henry's Public Relations 'creative team' had produced an artistic brochure full of glossy photographs of shiny, happy people with an introduction by Henry Vulture himself declaring that the project would provide 'sustainable, carbon-neutral development which would bring lasting benefits to the whole region'.

At a press conference to launch the scheme one spotty-faced youth from the local rag had the nerve to ask,

"Will there be any 'affordable housing'?"

"Certainly," Henry had replied reassuringly, adding under his breath, "affordable for the super-rich."

Henry's foot slipped on some wet grass. He stumbled and nearly fell. Horrid stuff, grass. Henry had no time for it. The golf course was going to be entirely covered with plastic turf. That would save a fortune in greenkeepers' wages for a start.

As he was strolling through the village, Henry noticed that a noisy mob had gathered by the churchyard wall. He went closer and saw, to his horror, that an almost-naked young man was slumped against the wall, covered in blood. The surrounding crowd were throwing stones at him. The missiles thumped into his flesh with a sickening thud. Soon the young man slid to the ground and lay very still.

Rather shaken, Henry walked away from the grisly spectacle. Although, during his business career, Henry had stabbed many rivals in the back, they had been metaphorical woundings carried out in the comfort of a plush City boardroom. The sight of real blood always upset him.

A few moments later, Henry's attention was attracted by a strange sight in a nearby field. His curiosity overcame his reluctance to get his shoes dirty and he went over to see what the bizarre object was. It turned out to be a large cross to which a man was nailed, upside down. His inverted head was on a level with Henry's.

"Afternoon, sir," said the man. "Nice day, but I think we might have a few showers later."

Henry was hurrying back towards the road when his already frayed nerves were further shattered by a blood-curdling scream. Though horrified, he had to find out where such a heart-rending screech was coming from. He didn't have far to go. About a hundred yards up the road, fixed to a wooden post, was a huge wheel, larger than a cartwheel. Around the rim, pointing outwards, were sharp metal spikes.

Lying on top of the wheel was a young woman in a white dress. One man was tugging at her feet and another was pulling her arms almost out of their sockets causing the unfortunate girl's body to stretch and the metal spikes to bite deeply into her back. This refinement to her torture led to the woman's shrieks and pleas for mercy becoming even more strident.

Henry had seen enough. He turned round and hurried back towards the safety of his car. As he passed the churchyard wall, he noticed that the crowd had dispersed but the young man was still lying on the ground in a crumpled heap. He soon discovered where the people had gone. As he looked along a side street he saw a bonfire – no, correction, TWO bonfires.

As he got closer, Henry discerned that these were no ordinary bonfires. What had he expected? In the middle of each conflagration was an elderly man, grey-haired and grey-bearded, wearing religious vestments and tied to a stake. They seemed to be muttering prayers and their hands were clasped together in gestures of supplication. As the flames crackled higher, one of them called out in a loud voice. Henry couldn't hear clearly exactly what the man shouted but it seemed to be something about lighting a candle. What an extraordinary remark in the circumstances! However it seemed to impress the watching throng because they responded with a mixture of jeers, catcalls, whistles and mocking laughter.

A disgusting old crone who was wearing a filthy black dress and had long straggly hair, a hook nose and pox-scarred face reached into one of the fires with a pointed stick and speared what appeared to be a very small burnt sausage. She offered the morsel to Henry.

"Care for a roast slug, sir?"

Henry shook his head.

"Only trying to be friendly," said the hag. She placed the roast slug in her mouth and chewed with relish. "Delicious!"

Henry had intended to have lunch at the local pub but now found that he had quite lost his appetite.

He hurried back to the Jag and climbed into the driver's seat. His hands were shaking and, though it was a chilly day, he was bathed in sweat. He rested his head on the steering wheel and closed his eyes. Henry wasn't going to abandon his grandiose development plans but wherever he eventually built his multi-million pound leisure complex, it wouldn't be in Tolpuddle.

As Henry Vulture was beating a hasty retreat from his rural nightmare and speeding towards the cosiness of the metropolis, the bar of the village inn was alive with excited chatter.

"I'm getting a bit old for this," said *St Peter*. "All that blood rushing to my head can't be doing me any good."

"And I'm in agony!" complained *St Catherine*. "That wheel nearly broke my back."

"It's MEANT to!" smirked the young man who had been tugging at *St Catherine's* feet. "AND you were overdoing it as usual."

"I was NOT!" denied *St Catherine* hotly. A tall, dark-haired, good-looking girl she had dreams of being 'discovered' by a Hollywood talent scout.

"Anyway," continued the young man, "St Catherine was a virgin. That really WOULD test your acting skills!"

"Now then children," said *St Peter* as *St Catherine* gave the young man a resounding slap in the face.

Meanwhile, *Bishop Latimer* was sitting at a table, his false beard still smouldering, with his feet in a bucket of ice.

"Give us a blessing, Bish," requested a cheeky teenager who had been one of the jeering crowd gathered round the bonfires. *Bishop Latimer* made a very unclerical remark.

Leaning on the bar, *St Stephen,* caked in fake blood, gratefully sank his first pint of *Piddle* in one gulp.

"Well done, boys and girls. Great show!" said *St Peter* in his Dorset accent. "We've well and truly scared off that London busybody. Somehow, I don't think he will be constructing his luxury homes and golf course in Tolpuddle. But, remember we have to do all this again next Tuesday."

"Oh God!" exclaimed *St Catherine*. "Who is it this time?"

"A coachload of Americans."

"Don't tell me *YANKEE-DOODLE TOURS* have put Tolpuddle back on the agenda for *Dorset in two-and-a-half Hours?*" groaned *Bishop Latimer*.

"I'm afraid so," said *St Peter*. "I know we thought we had seen them off – but that was three years ago. The firm is now *Under New Management.* We need to put on another convincing performance. Frighten the living daylights out of them. Perhaps then they WILL go away for good. So let's make it really gruesome. Buckets of gore and don't stint on the paraffin!"

Bishop Latimer made an even more unclerical remark.

"Keep an eye on the middle-aged women," pleaded *St Stephen*. "The blue-rinse brigade really lap-up the violence. Last time a couple of them joined in the stoning – using real stones." He winced at the memory.

"By the way, where were the real *Tolpuddle Martyrs?* They are normally part of the display," asked *Bishop Latimer*. "You remember, a bedraggled group of agricultural labourers, manacled together being driven along by a vicious overseer in a top hat, cracking a whip. I didn't see them today."

"That's because they weren't here," replied *St Peter*. "And you won't be seeing them in the future. They've gone away."

"What do you mean. Gone away?"

"Hadn't you heard?" said *St Peter*. "They have been transported to Australia."

Memorandum

To   Managing Editor

From   Chief Weather Forecaster

I must confess that I was somewhat surprised to receive your memorandum dated August 24th. As managing editor of the radio station, you have a right to state your views but to describe my department as 'worse than useless' is, I think, unfair and you go on to say that 'despite spending a vast amount of money on the latest equipment' we 'failed to get one prediction correct' concerning 'this complete washout of a summer' and that you would be better off 'employing a half-trained chimpanzee with a piece of damp seaweed'. I agree that I hold the post of Chief Weather Forecaster, as you so kindly put it 'for the time being' but that doesn't mean I can tell in advance what is going to happen. Who do you think I am? Mystic Meg?

If I may deal with the specific points you have raised

1) The summer has not been a 'complete washout'. In fact, the sun shone for a total of 39 minutes at Stoke-on-Trent on 3rd August.

2) Concerning the widespread flooding that has left East Anglia entirely submerged. Our forecast was 'Showers developing, some prolonged'. Note those words. I would certainly argue that continuous rain for forty days and forty nights comes within the category of 'a prolonged shower'. Besides the situation is not as bad as has been portrayed. There have been sightings of a large wooden boat floating on the waters with many animals on board.

3) I admit we did not adequately predict the arrival of an ice age in Scotland. This was the result of human error. The forecast which should have been broadcast was 'It will be rather chilly in Scotland with below average temperatures'. I think you will agree that -27°c is a 'below average temperature' for July – even in Aberdeen. However that was not the forecast which went out. One of my assistants pressed a wrong button on the computer so we issued a heatwave warning and advised people to carry a bottle of water with them. Unfortunately, the water in those bottles has frozen solid. Anyway, Scottish people have less to complain about now as for the past three weeks molten lava has been cascading down the slopes of Ben Nevis to keep them warm. Of course we knew that Ben Nevis was an active volcano about to erupt at any moment but we withheld the information for fear it might cause mass hysteria and widespread panic. That isn't strictly true. I wanted to tell people that Ben Nevis was about to erupt and thereby cause mass hysteria and widespread panic but was overruled by my superiors.

4) Regarding the plague of locusts which descended on Somerset last month, I admit that we did not use the precise term 'plague of locusts'. But we did warn that 'there are a lot of nasty creepy crawlies about at this time of year' and advised people to lay in stocks of insect repellent. It is not our fault if the insect repellent was ineffective.

5) I do not consider slaughter of the first born to be a meteorological phenomenon and therefore take no responsibility for failing to predict it.

6) I am already working on your suggestions and have arranged for a quantity of seaweed to be gathered from Weymouth beach. I have also contacted Monkey World with regard to their supplying a half-trained chimpanzee.

7) There are still three days left of official summer. It is therefore possible that the sun might come out to redeem what has been, I admit, a disappointing few months. Then again, it might not. That's the thing with the British weather, you can never forecast what it is going to be like, can you? I certainly can't.

Art for Art's Sake

The weather was bitter as they crossed the barren landscape, hunched in their cloaks, following that distant star. Mostly, they remained silent. Perhaps they were reflecting on the strangeness of their journey. They weren't intrepid adventurers but kings, accustomed to command. They travelled alone, these powerful men, who had previously gone nowhere without a vast retinue of servants. They had abandoned their lives of luxury, their ornate palaces, their scheming ministers, their hard-eyed wives, their teenage concubines. And all because of a star.

They travelled at night, stopping each morning at remote inns where locals eyed them with sullen envy. These kings were accustomed to have paid ruffians to guard them while they ate and slept. Now, with no protection, they feared for their possessions and even their lives.

And always the weather was turning colder. Never had anyone known winters as bleak as this. One night, they were caught by a fierce blizzard. Unable to see the star, or make any headway in such conditions, they huddled together next to the camels to try to keep warm. When the weather cleared, they were shivering and soaked to the skin. The other two feared for Caspar but that frail old man was tougher than he looked. After all, he hadn't been born royal but had seized power after leading a bloody rebellion.

The camels were worse affected. All three began coughing and sneezing, their progress slowed to a plod and soon they were hardly able to put one hoof in front of another. The oriental monarchs were not experts in infectious diseases but it would have made no difference if they had been. Their animals were suffering from a particularly virulent strain of camel 'flu which is nearly always fatal. And so it proved. Very soon each beast keeled over in turn and breathed its last.

"What do we do now?" asked Balthazar.

"We walk, young man," replied Caspar.

"I never walk anywhere," said Balthazar arrogantly. "I employ servants to do my walking for me."

"What is he saying?" enquired Caspar, who was rather deaf. "He employs servants to do his wanking for him. I would never do that, it spoils the fun."

These pampered aristocrats had no choice but to complete their journey on foot. They had only been going for a few hours, though to them it felt like a lot longer, when they spied, grazing on some rough grass, a herd of wild creatures, like horses, only smaller and covered in black and white stripes.

"What are those?" asked Balthazar.

"They're zebras, my boy," answered Caspar.

"Can we ride them?"

"I don't think we have much choice," said Caspar.

Admittedly, it took some time to master the technique and each of them fell off several times except Caspar, who seemed perfectly at ease. Even when they had become almost proficient, these zebra-mounted kings were a rather comical sight.

That year, Judean artists had never had it so good. There was so much work available that just about anyone who could hold a brush was given a commission. The whole process had started months ago with the Annunciation. Then there had been the innkeeper turning the young couple away; the angel appearing to the shepherds; the stable scene when the shepherds arrived to worship the infant child. Now it was time for the arrival of the wise men and another interior stable scene showing the magi paying homage to the infant Jesus. All this and there was the *Flight into Egypt* and the *Massacre of the Innocents* still to come.

The artist who had got the job of recording the arrival of the kings was a fierce-looking young man who fancied himself as something of a rebel. He set up his easel about a quarter of a mile from the stable on the route the magi were sure to take. He knew he wouldn't have much time as they were busy men. So he sketched in the background and waited.

As soon as the kings came into view on the horizon the artist began to work furiously. As an ardent republican, he had little respect for royalty but this was paid work and he needed the money. He had nearly finished his preliminary study by the time the wise men reached him. Eager to get a glimpse, they dismounted (or rather slithered off their zebras) and went to inspect the drawing.

Balthazar was the youngest and most hot-tempered of the kings. He was not pleased with what he saw.

"What do you mean by this?" he shouted and was about to grab the canvas and fling it on the ground when Melchior put a restraining hand on his arm.

Balthazar stepped back and Melchior spoke to the artist in a soothing tone.

"That's a very fine drawing. Most lifelike. But there is one small problem. We were supposed to arrive by camel but, owing to unforeseen circumstances we were forced to use these – er - zebras. I don't want to compromise your artistic integrity. I'm sure, though, that it would be much better for everyone if you were to paint us riding, not zebras, but camels as was intended."

"I'm sorry," replied the artist. "I paint what I see. As you are riding zebras, I will have to paint you riding zebras."

"We are wasting our time with this fellow," interrupted Balthazar angrily. "Let's hang him upside down from the nearest tree and chop off his hands. He will soon come to his senses then."

"If we chop off his hands we won't get our painting," pointed out Melchior. He turned to the artist, reached into his leather purse, took out two gold coins and placed them on a nearby rock. "My dear chap, can't you use your imagination? Surely you can draw a camel."

"Of course I can draw a camel. At the Jerusalem School of Art we drew nothing but fucking camels for months on end. But, I repeat. If I see zebras, I have to put zebras in my picture."

Melchior placed two more gold coins on the rock.

"You must admit that the camel is a magnificent animal, the ship of the desert. What a painting it would make, the three of us, dressed in flowing robes, emerging from the desert at dusk, mounted on our faithful camels. But, as for zebras? To be honest, if I was at home, cruising along the highway in my state coach, I wouldn't even bother to stop if I saw a zebra crossing."

The artist didn't reply. Melchior could see that the artist was eyeing the coins covetously. The Arabian king sighed. Every man had his price. Very slowly, he took out four more coins and placed them on the rock. The artist couldn't take his eyes off them. These coins weren't of the debased local currency, with Caesar's head on them, but mysterious oriental money and they were solid gold. There was a fortune on the rock, enough to fund a luxurious lifestyle and keep him in wine, women and psalms for years. Finally, he spoke.

"As you say, an artist sometimes has to use his imagination and, when you think of it a zebra is a most unattractive animal. I shall paint you three wise men, wearing flowing robes, emerging from the desert at dusk riding – camels."

And, as we know, he did.

The Girl on the Train

The train, which had been crowded when we left Waterloo, was now almost empty. I dozed off for a few moments. When I woke, I reached forward and put my hand over the back of the seat in front of me. I touched someone's hair.

"I'm sorry," I said.

"That's quite all right," a girl's voice replied. "We are alone in the carriage. Come and sit beside me?"

I moved forward. The seat in front of me appeared to be empty but I sat down on the side nearest the gangway. Though I couldn't see the girl, I could sense her presence. She lay her head on my shoulder. I reached across with my right arm, turning towards her. I must have looked ridiculous embracing an empty seat but I knew the girl was real. I kissed her, taking my time. We remained like that for a few moments. Then the train slowed.

"This is my stop. Will I -"

"Will you see me again? But you haven't seen me for the first time, yet, have you?"

That was true.

"The answer is 'maybe'. For obvious reasons, you won't be able to find me. I will find you."

I have travelled on that train frequently and though, on several occasions, I've been alone in a carriage, the girl hasn't found me. Once I thought a soft hand stroked my arm and once I felt someone unseen push past me but I might have been imagining things.

When Hannibal was planning military strategy at a meeting of his commanders, no-one mentioned the elephant in the room.

A Cup of Coffee with Anne Boleyn

She was already twenty minutes late but what had I expected? She was a very busy lady indeed and I doubt I was very high on her list of priorities. I had chosen a seat at the back where perhaps we could have a conversation without being overheard. She was *half an hour* late by the time she dashed through the door. She was no conventional beauty. Her face was small, oval-shaped and she had a long swan-like neck but there was something about her that made people look up when she entered. Of course, a lot of the customers in that coffee-shop might have recognised her as by then she was quite famous – some would say notorious.

I'm old enough now to complain about the 'modern woman'. How they rush about everywhere hardly pausing for breath – not like the elegant ladies of my youth.

She didn't see me at first and looked about her for a moment or two, rather confused. I smiled. I knew she was short sighted but too vain to wear glasses.

"Oh *there* you are. Hiding from me were you? So sorry I'm late, but I haven't stopped this morning. Honestly life these days is just one long whirl. I'm glad to get off my feet for five minutes."

As I said 'the modern woman'.

When the waitress arrived, Anne ordered a latte and a pain au chocolat. "I'm starving."

We sat in silence for a few moments. Even at 11.30am, the place wasn't too busy. I didn't think we would be overheard.

"He won't marry you," I said. "You do realise that."

"Wow. Nothing like coming straight to the point."

"I've known him a long time. And I repeat, he won't marry you."

"What you mean is that you and people who think like you won't recognise the marriage."

"No, I mean he won't go through any form of marriage

ceremony with you. He is at heart a very moral man, a religious man-"

"But he's had loads of mistresses," she interrupted. "Including my own sister."

"And you will just be one more on the list. When I say he's a religious man, I mean he believes that in God's eyes he's married to Katherine and always will be."

"He quotes Leviticus-"

"I know he does. He's trying to convince himself as much as anything. But his conscience won't allow him to divorce Katherine. And he does have a conscience despite what people think."

"You are forgetting one very important thing. Henry desperately wants to screw me. Honestly he's like a bull in heat and I'm not going to let him fuck me unless he marries me."

So much for being discreet. Anne's voice might not have been loud but it carried a long way – we had everyone's attention now. A middle-aged lady pouring tea for her mother at a neighbouring table just kept on pouring even though the cup was full. A rather spotty youth swallowed half his cappuccino in one gulp and two teenage girls forgot about their banana smoothies and stared at us with mouths open and eyes wide as saucers. Anne carried on regardless.

"Furthermore, he needs a son to succeed him, a legitimate son not a royal bastard. Katherine is too old to have any more children – any more monsters," she giggled. "So, for reasons of state, he has to marry someone and why not me? I can give him a son."

"There's Mary," I said.

"Mary's a girl, in case you hadn't noticed. A woman can't control an unruly kingdom like England. It takes a man, a real man."

"Nevertheless, if it is God's will that Mary should succeed him, Henry will just have to accept it."

"Henry won't accept it and I won't accept it," she declared, her eyes flashing with defiance. Then she put her hand on mine and looking me full in the face said quietly, "I *am* going to marry Henry and I *am* going to be queen."

She saw me glancing at the very expensive Cartier watch she was wearing. "Yes, that was a present, a birthday present. Though Henry didn't actually pay for it. We saw the watch in a jeweller's window and went inside the shop. Henry asked to be shown the watch then just took it – the man behind the counter didn't dare ask for money. Oh is that the time? I'm late for the hairdresser. I must fly." She gave me a quick kiss on the forehead and rushed out of the restaurant.

I watched her go. She was twenty-seven but seemed like an eager schoolgirl. For all the veneer and polish of her French education she was quite innocent of the ways of the world. Yet some saw her as a *femme fatale*. I shook my head. Anne would be much better advised to accept the role of the king's mistress – by aiming to be queen she was playing for very high stakes. You see, I might be wrong. Henry might well go through a form of marriage with her 'for reasons of state'. A marriage which I could never acknowledge. I have seen enough of kings to know that monarchs live by different rules from other men. They have to.

"I can give him a son." But supposing she couldn't. What then? She might well be in great danger. I had a premonition that some awful fate awaited Anne Boleyn.

Anne had left me to pick up the tab as usual. Even in these days, a title does count for something. I saw the girl on the till look at me with added respect as she read the name *Sir Thomas More* on my Barclaycard.

Relaxing in the bath, Archimedes sensed he was on the verge of a great discovery. Then he accidentally pulled out the plug with his toe and the water drained away.

The Answering Machine

Let me admit straightaway that it was my mistake – a very small mistake, it is true but the consequences were rather dramatic.

I was about to set off on a three week Sunday Times Wine Club Holiday in France and my friends advised me to buy an answering machine before I went. All this was a good many years ago when even mobile phones, though they had, regrettably, been invented, were by no means common, certainly not as universal as they have now become, bringing, in my opinion, just about as much benefit to the human race as the Black Death. If I had known what further horrors were about to be inflicted on us, such as Google, e-bay, i-Pads, tablets, Facebook and Twitter, I would have thrown myself off the ferry before it was even half way across the Channel.

Before I departed, I plugged in my new answering machine and got the thing, I thought, working correctly. I enjoyed the holiday immensely. However, I found myself in disagreement with other members of the group. Their method of appreciating wine was to sniff the glass for a few moments, take a small sip, roll the liquid round their mouth then spit it out. I, on the other hand, would pour the stuff into the pewter pint tankard I had thoughtfully brought with me, take a deep breath and swallow the lot in one gulp. To my mind, you can only really appreciate a good wine after you have downed about eight bottles. I also became involved in a dispute with the tour company. I argued that I was entitled to a substantial refund because I had never used the luxury en-suite accommodation they provided as I had spent every night of my holiday lying unconscious on the filthy floor of some squalid estaminet. Further unpleasantness occurred when no-one was willing to sit next to me on the coach – though I do admit that this might have been due to my habit of breakfasting on a litre of Beaujolais and three cloves of raw garlic.

Despite these little local difficulties, I returned home relaxed and refreshed and, as I climbed the stairs to my flat, I was looking forward to getting stuck into the many bottles of duty free which were clanking in my rucksack. My apartment is the only one on the fourth floor and I live in a fairly quiet neighbourhood, so I was surprised to see a number of people on the landing, apparently waiting for me.

There was a young man, dressed in a short tunic. He was well-muscled and athletic, almost god-like in appearance. He had on a winged helmet and sandals, which also had wings on them, and he carried a staff. That had wings as well and two live snakes wound round it. Next to him was a military figure in khaki uniform, standing next to a rather old-fashioned, mud-spattered motorcycle. A scruffy-looking ragamuffin of about fourteen was sitting astride a butcher's bike. You know, the ones that have a large wicker-basket and a small front wheel. Then there was a boy of about the same age but who was wearing a smart blue uniform with a peaked cap.

There were two women amongst the group. Both, I would say in their mid-twenties but with contrasting appearances. One was demurely dressed in a long-sleeved white blouse and a black knee-length skirt. With her spectacles and dark hair tied in a neat pony-tail, she seemed the perfect picture of an efficient secretary. The other, who had a shock of obviously dyed blonde hair was heavily made up with cherry red lipstick. She was wearing a halter-neck silver gown which showed off her ample cleavage and could easily be taken for a 1950s film star.

Oh, I almost forgot. A bird was sitting on the window-sill with something tied round one of its legs. I'm not very good at identifying birds but this looked to me like some kind of dove.

Though all these people had been waiting patiently, as soon as they saw me they all started talking at the same time. I couldn't hear what anyone was saying – though I did notice the urchin lad nudge the boy in the blue uniform and, eyeing up the platinum blonde, remark, "I couldn't 'arf give 'er one."

"Quiet, please," I shouted. "Now will you each speak in turn."

The man in khaki stood up ramrod straight and saluted. "Private Smith, despatch rider, *Royal Corps of Signals* at your service, sah!" Then the scruffy boy sniffed, wiped his nose on his sleeve and handed me a screwed-up piece of paper while the smart boy presented me with a brown envelope which, when I opened it turned out to be something called a 'telegram'. I had to rack my brains to recall what sort of communication that was. The athletic young man began speaking in a foreign language but I couldn't understand what he was saying – it was all Greek to me.

The efficient young lady handed me a typed sheet of A4 paper and spoke in a businesslike manner. "This is rather urgent. Will there be any reply?" The sexy young lady came close and whispered in my ear in a sultry voice. I won't repeat what she said except to remark that I hadn't got a gun in my pocket, I was pleased to see her and I would need to consume several bottles of my duty-free Beaujolais in order to gain sufficient strength to take her up on her offer. And I am not going to describe what the bird did but it took me some time to clean myself up afterwards.

Eventually all my visitors left. Most of them went down the stairs and exited through the front door. The blonde bombshell, though, went *up* the stairs. She was evidently the new tenant of the apartment on the top floor and must have moved in while I was on holiday. And the god-like young man opened a window, jumped through it and flew away soaring over the treetops, disappearing into the distance. I am not sure what happened to the bird but there was a rumour that the lady in the flat below made it into a rather tasty pie.

So, at last I was able to get into my flat. When I checked my answering machine, I realised the mistake I had made and though, as I said, it was a trivial error and, considering it was the first time I had used the contraption, an understandable one, it did explain why there had been all those people waiting on the landing.

What I *should* have said, when I was making the recording that would be heard when my number was dialled was "I'm sorry, I can't come to the phone at the moment, please leave a *message*".

What I *actually* said was "I'm sorry, I can't come to the phone at the moment, please leave a *messenger*".

The Lion Tamer

As soon as he saw the Monday morning headline in the paper 'Ferocious lion rampages through town. Six people eaten this weekend', the Lyme Regis lion tamer knew he was in trouble. Sure enough he was summoned by the Council Leader.

"We don't need this kind of publicity. Especially at the start of the tourist season. How long have you been doing this job?"

"Eight months."

"It's not good enough. I'm going to sack you. Eight months and you haven't tamed the lion."

"Of course I haven't tamed the lion."

"Why haven't you?"

"Because once the lion has been tamed you won't need a lion tamer will you? And I will be out of a job."

"But as I am going to sack you, you will be out of a job anyway."

"I don't think sacking me is a good idea."

"Why not?"

"If you sack me you will have to employ another lion tamer and he won't tame the lion either because if he does *he* will be out of a job. You can sack me if you like and employ another lion tamer but if you do you will have a ferocious lion rampaging through the town eating people."

"I've already got a ferocious lion rampaging through the town eating people."

"I know. Quite a problem, isn't it?"

"What would you suggest?"

"I would suggest you give me a pay rise."

"Why should I give you a pay rise?"

"Because it's a dangerous business, is lion taming."

The Astronomer (Part One)

The Astronomer reached out his hand and spun the globe. Then he glanced down at his notebook. Dim evening light seeped through a small window into the dingy room. But he was certain. He didn't need to scan the heavens with a telescope any more. He had double-checked his calculations. This small-town nonentity, regarded as a harmless eccentric by most of his neighbours, had just made one of the great scientific discoveries of the Middle Ages. Years of dogged perseverance had been vindicated. He ought to have been a happy man but he wasn't because he knew that when he made his findings public, the wrath of the Holy Church would be unleashed against him – not a pleasant prospect. In fact, the Astronomer, a rather nervous person, frequently imagined he could hear the tread of weighty footsteps on the stairs as heavily-armed Soldiers of God came to arrest him and take him away to a stinking, rat-infested cell. The Astronomer was so deep in thought that he failed to notice a figure who was standing behind him, looking over his shoulder.

"My word, that's very good," said the newcomer who spoke in a cultivated, upper-class drawl. "I can't understand the whole thing but you seem to have hit the nail on the head." The Astronomer kept looking at the globe and didn't turn round. If he had, he would have seen that the individual who was speaking was naked from the waist up. His bald head had two horns growing out of the temple. He also had a long tail, cloven hoofs instead of feet and was carrying a three-pronged pitchfork.

"Yes, when you make your findings known, you will be one of the most famous men in the whole world."

"Maybe I will."

"There's no 'maybe' about it. You will be fêted everywhere you go, offered professorships at the best universities and paid a fortune to deliver incomprehensible three hour lectures to bone-headed students. Kings and emperors will hang on your every word. What is more, you will go down in history as a great scientist. All you have to do is make your findings widely known. What is stopping you?"

"The Church," replied the Astronomer. "My 'discovery' will challenge their teaching on the nature of the universe. The cardinals won't like that and they are not a forgiving crew. They will come after me with everything they have got. I don't want to be tortured. I don't want to be burnt at the stake. I don't want to be hauled before the Inquisition."

"Don't worry about the Church, old son, I never do. Yes, your discovery may well upset the boys in red and they will attempt to discredit you but, in the end, they will have to admit that you are right. And, don't forget you will be the most renowned scholar in Europe by then, so they will never dare harm you. No, take my advice, publish your conclusions and enjoy the well-deserved acclaim."

"I'll need to think about it. Anyway, it's late and I'm tired."

"Yes, I need to be off as well. I have many dastardly deeds to perform before I can get some shut-eye," said the visitor and walked out of the room. But the Devil hadn't been telling the truth. He didn't leave the Astronomer's house but hid in a broom cupboard. And when the Astronomer had retired to bed, the corrupter-in-chief of humanity returned to the study.

Working quickly, by the light of a flickering candle, the Devil copied figures and equations from the notebook onto a scroll of paper, an evil grin on his face the whole time, as he realised how much trouble this information was going to cause.

At 3am, all was quiet in the Palazzo Torquemada, the headquarters of the Spanish Inquisition. But in a small room, high in the building, a powerfully built, dark-haired middle-aged man in a red robe was waiting impatiently. Eventually the door opened and the Devil walked in.

"So you are here at last – about bloody time."

"My sincere apologies, Cardinal Enchilada. But there is so much wickedness in the world these days that I have my work cut out to keep track of it all. Anyway, I've managed to get hold of the material you require. Pretty powerful stuff, I'd say. Take a look."

He handed over the scroll on which he had copied the information from the Astronomer's notebook.

"Yes, it's all here. You've done well, Nick."

As it *was* 3am and Enchilada was still wearing his cardinal's robes, the Devil wondered if he slept in them. As a matter of fact, he did. His mistress, a Carmelite nun, got a real thrill out of fucking a cardinal dressed as a cardinal.

"How goes our scheme?" asked the Devil.

"It goes well."

"Remember that we have a deal."

"I remember," said the cardinal.

"Good. I think we will make a jolly good team, Cardinal Enchilada, you and I," said the Devil.

"I am sure we will. Especially since, despite appearances, we are actually on the same side."

The Astronomer's fears proved justified. That afternoon he heard the tread of weighty footsteps on the stairs as heavily-armed Soldiers of God came to arrest him and take him away to a stinking, rat-infested cell.

A few days later, three men in red robes were sitting behind a table in the room where the cardinal had met the Devil. In the middle was Enchilada. To his right a very thin man with a ghostly pale face and wild, staring eyes. He had two fang-like teeth and blood running down his chin. On Enchilada's left was a fat man slumped in his seat. He was breathing noisily and appeared to be asleep.

The Astronomer was standing, head bowed, in front of this strange triumvirate.

"You know why you are here?" asked Enchilada.

"I really have no idea, your eminence. I am a simple scholar, engaged in obscure academic research. I am no danger to anybody."

"Bollocks," retorted Cardinal Enchilada. "Your 'obscure academic research' has led to certain conclusions, has it not? Conclusions which are in direct conflict with the teachings of the Holy Church. Conclusions which amount to heresy."

"I assure you that I have come to no such conclusions. I am merely a humble stargazer."

"Do you deny that you have formed a theory, a ludicrous and implausible theory, that, instead of being the fixed centre of the universe around which the stars, moon, sun, planets and all celestial bodies revolve, the Earth itself circles round the sun in a 'so-called' orbit?"

"I repeat, Your Eminence, that I merely note what I observe, I do not -"

"God give me strength!" yelled Enchilada. "You would try the patience of a saint and I'm no saint. Well, my brothers, what shall we do with this miserable specimen? Any ideas?"

"Burn him. Burn him at the stake. He will confess then," urged the cardinal with the long fangs and the blood running down his chin.

"He can hardly confess if he's dead, can he, Cardinal Dracula?" remarked Enchilada. "Cardinal Wolsey what do you have to say?"

The fat man opened his eyes, looked round him and spoke in a sad voice. "Had I served my God with half the zeal I served my king, He would in mine age not have left me naked to face mine enemies."

"You don't look naked to me," observed Cardinal Dracula. "That's a fine piece of cloth you are wearing. If you don't want it, I'll have it. You can get a good price for genuine second hand cardinal's robes at certain places I know, provided you don't ask any awkward questions. But come on, Enchilada, don't be such a grumpy old spoilsport. If you won't let us burn the astronomer, at least we can put him on the rack or use the thumbscrews on him. I just *love* the thumbscrews. We wouldn't even have to employ a professional sadist. I would willingly operate the screws myself."

"I don't think so," said Cardinal Enchilada. "We aren't going to subject the Astronomer to any sort of physical abuse. The Inquisition is respected throughout Christendom as an exceptionally benign institution. We will instead return this trouble-maker to his stinking, rat-infested cell there to remain in total darkness and exist on a diet of bread and water. It will, of course, be rotting, mildewed bread scavenged from the municipal rubbish dump and waste water from the morgue in which plague-ridden bodies have been washed. We will interview him again in a week's time."

"But will he talk then?" asked Cardinal Wolsey.

"Oh, he'll talk alright. We have ways of making people talk."

The Balloon

"Name please," said the psychiatrist as the next patient settled down on the couch.

"Ivan."

"Oh God, not another Russian Czar. Already this month, I've had five Peters, three Alexanders and a Catherine. Why can't it be like the old days when everyone thought they were Napoleon?"

"No. I don't believe I'm a Russian Czar. Ivan's my name. My real name."

"I see, so what is your problem?"

"I think I'm a balloon."

"Helium or hot air?"

"Helium."

"That's not so terrible. To fly up beyond the earth's atmosphere to the very edge of space. What tremendous views you must get."

"I'm not that kind of balloon. I'm moored in the leisure gardens in a seaside resort. I'm fixed to a strong cable 500 feet long and I have to go up and down all day taking holiday makers 'sightseeing'. "Don't those people look small? Ooh is that the Isle of Wight?" And I have to put up with their whining sticky fingered kids who often end up being sick in my basket. What a life. I just can't take any more."

"This is a difficult case. I think we will have to call a special conference to decide your future."

Meanwhile, and you have to remember that Ivan was a patient in a mental hospital in the 1950s, he was put under restraint. Ivan's arms and legs were tied to the bed and a rope wrapped round his chest. To stop him floating away, I guess.

Lucky for Some

"He's very quiet."

"He's always quiet."

"But not *this* quiet. You haven't had a row, have you? He always sulks when you have had a row."

"Not really. I mean, no more than usual."

The voices were coming from behind me as I sat on a train steaming north so I couldn't see the speakers. In fact, I never did see them. The voices were both female. One voice was of an older woman, aged about fifty, I would guess, and the other of a person in her mid twenties.

"He's *very* quiet." The younger voice.

Silence.

"Oh no, Mum. He's -" The younger voice again. Surprised. Agitated.

"Yes, dear." The older voice, soothing. "I've known for quite a long time."

"How long?"

"Since Wolverhampton."

"So, what are we going to do? We've got to change at Crewe."

"Yes, I know, dear."

"Oh, Mum, you don't mean- we can't just *leave* him."

"Look Carole, we have to be practical. We can hardly take your dad with us. We've a lot of luggage as it is and you can never find a porter on a station platform these days."

"But this train goes to Manchester. He *hates* Manchester."

"That's not going to bother him now, though, is it?"

Another period of silence followed. A rather strained silence, I thought. Then the train slowed.

"We're here." The older voice. "I think you will need your coat, Carole. It's a bit nippy today."

A sigh and then the younger voice, "Oh, well, Mum. I suppose you are right."

"I usually am, dear."

The two women got off the train. My curiosity was thoroughly aroused. Of the four seats around the table where the women had been sitting, only one was occupied and that was by a middle-aged gentleman wearing a grey suit and fawn raincoat. As Carole had remarked, he was quiet, very quiet. And the reason for his silence was soon obvious. The man was dead. I must admit that, for a moment I succumbed to a most unchivalrous thought. I suspected that the two ladies might have murdered him. But I soon realised that this was not the case for, if they *had* planned murder, they would have made better arrangements for the disposal of the body. The overheard conversation indicated that the man's death had not been foreseen but had come as a surprise to them and they were at a loss what to do.

As the older lady had said, they couldn't take both the luggage and their deceased relative with them so, very sensibly, they had chosen to take the luggage.

Strictly speaking, none of this was any of my business but knowing the ways of British Rail as I did, I was well aware that the poor chap might be left in this grimy train for weeks or even months, travelling between Euston and Manchester Piccadilly, before any member of staff took action. He deserved better than that.

The next stop was Stockport. When the train came to a halt, I slung the uncomplaining corpse over my shoulder and stepped out on to the platform. As it was early Saturday afternoon the station wasn't very crowded and I soon found a bench on which I could place my inert companion. Not that the seat was unoccupied – there were several others there already and, like my new-found friend, they were all very quiet.

I was glad that this was happening on a cold April day as, quite frankly, some of the occupants of the bench were in a rather unhygienic condition. If they were still there in the summer – and they probably would be – flies and bluebottles would be swarming all over them. This wouldn't happen to the bloke at the very end, though, because he was merely a skeleton dressed in tattered rags. Clearly, he had been there for quite a time. But, in reality, not much longer than most people had to wait for a British Rail train in the 1960s.

I walked out of the station and into the nearest pub for a drink. I thought I had earned a beer. As I was sipping my pint, one thing puzzled me about the behaviour of the two ladies. Why hadn't they taken his wallet? The first thing I'd done was to go through the dead man's pockets – it was only natural. There wasn't a lot of money, only a few pounds but that would go quite a long way in those days. In fact the cash from the wallet was paying for the ale I was drinking. I lifted my glass to the benefactor I had never met. Well, never met while he was alive. "Cheers, mate."

As well as the money, there had been a betting-slip in the wallet. The Grand National was being run that day and I was quite excited on discovering the slip until I saw the name of the horse. A lot of luck is associated with the National and people say that any horse can win. That is largely true but there *are* exceptions and this was one. The animal my late friend had backed was priced at 100/1 but, for all the chance it had, 1000/1 would have been more realistic odds. In fact, I was going to screw up the slip and throw it into the fire but the race was about to start – it was being shown on the TV in the pub and I settled down to watch what turned out to be one of the most famous or rather, most notorious, Grand Nationals ever.

At the fence after Becher's Brook, on the second circuit, a loose horse, instead of jumping the obstacle, turned sideways and ran across the track bringing down several of the leading horses. The rest of the field crashed into these. There was an almighty pile-up and soon every horse had either fallen or unseated its rider – with the exception of one. This creature was so slow and so far behind all the others that his jockey was able to steer clear of the carnage, jump the fence and go on to win. And the name of the horse was the name on the betting slip in front of me. FOINAVON. Two quid each way at 100/1. That came to over £250. A lot of money in 1967.

That's racing for you. The dead bloke can't have known anything about the sport or else he would never have backed such a no-hoper. The result was a complete fluke. I fancied myself as something of an expert – I lost money in the bookies nearly every day. But the horse I had bet on (after studying form with great care) had got caught in the pile-up and never finished, yet *his* complete outsider had won. Some people have all the luck.

Normally, I am quite upset when a horse I have backed loses; sometimes I'm inconsolable for almost 10 minutes. But today things didn't seem so bad. I accepted my fate philosophically. It was warm in the pub and I was in no hurry. True, I needed to go to the bookies and collect my Foinavon cash. Well, strictly speaking, the stranger's Foinavon cash but he wouldn't have much use for it would he? And I wanted to get to Marks and Spencer's before they closed to buy a shirt as the polyester jumper was starting to irritate my skin. It was the first time I had ever made a profit from a British Rail journey. I almost felt guilty about dodging the fare. I ordered another pint and, as a shower of hail rattled against the windowpane, I began planning a holiday in the sun.

Armour of a Fool

I've never liked the night before a battle. Some leaders prefer to remain quietly on their own, contemplating the morrow but this king, drunken sot that he was, preferred to feast so, of course, I had to put on a show. Not that he was a real king, not any more. He had been deposed seven years ago but we all had still to bow and scrape and refer to him as 'Your Majesty'.

On these occasions, there is only one thing to do; be as crude as possible. Subtlety is never much in demand from court jesters but when most people's minds are elsewhere coarse lavatorial humour and blatant sexual innuendo (together with appropriate gestures) are what is needed. Not everyone was pleased. One or two who had been scowling throughout my act, clearly weren't amused and ostentatiously walked out. That showed how our 'king' was losing his grip. They wouldn't have dared do that a few years ago.

Afterwards, the various commanders left to go about their business. Many would turn to God and pray for, if not victory, at least for survival. Not all though. The camp whores would do good trade and not only in the sense of being well paid for services rendered. This was a rare chance for the more enterprising to rob their client while he slept, knowing that when he awoke he would be too busy with more important matters to chase after them.

One who clearly was going to use the services of the ladies of easy virtue was Sir John Hogston, a scarred veteran of many campaigns who had been ransomed at least twice. "If this is to be my last night on Earth I intend to spend most of it fucking," he declared.

"Don't look so shocked, Reverend." This remark was addressed to a bishop who had overheard him. "I'll make time to pray as well. In fact these days I often find myself praying while I'm shagging."

"Woe betide the trollop who tries to make off with *his* purse," I thought.

The 'king' who had been the life and soul of the party half an hour before was now sunk in melancholy. I wasn't surprised. He had a lot to lose if things went badly tomorrow. Come to think of if, so did I. The rebellion had started promisingly. People had become disillusioned with the ruler who deposed our 'good old king' and had embarked on a series of reckless foreign adventures, exacting high taxes to pay for them. A ruler who had neglected his own country and allowed gangs of robbers and vagabonds to terrorise the realm. There had also been a series of bad harvests and a return of the plague for which the reigning monarch was always blamed. Many had yearned for the (seemingly) better days of the 'good old king'. And when he had returned from exile and landed on the west coast, crowds had flocked to support him. But the 'good old king' had dithered. He had wasted time. Instead of making a quick march on the capital, he had enjoyed a rather leisurely tour of those regions loyal to him, accepting their homage. This had allowed his opponent to regroup and gather his forces. What, only a few weeks ago, had appeared certain to be a successful campaign now had the stench of defeat. And tomorrow the battle would be fought that would decide the issue.

What would happen if that battle was lost? The 'good old king' if not killed outright would certainly be captured. He wouldn't be allowed to go into exile again. He would be shut up in some grim fortress – but not for long. Within a few months, at most, an 'unfortunate accident' would happen. He might expire for lack of water or a jailer, seduced by clinking coins, would smother him in his sleep. Maybe he would suffer a more gruesome end. But suffer an end he would. No country can accommodate two living kings.

The rest of us would have to fend for ourselves as best we could. We would probably have to run for our lives. Then for me it would be a return to the open road, the troubadour life, not something to look forward to. Out in all weathers, the wind, the cold, the rain, the snow. Travelling from town to town in my threadbare motley, often soaked to the skin. Trying to attract a meagre crowd and persuade them to part with their hard-earned money by telling jokes, dancing, singing, behaving more like a performing monkey than a human being. A difficult enough life for a young man in times of plenty but for someone of my age, adrift in a resentful, morose land, an existence to be avoided if at all possible.

That explains why I was still in the camp – why I hadn't run away already. Battles are never entirely predictable. With soldiers of the calibre of Sir John Hogston there was always a chance of victory and the 'good old king' was an impressive military commander when he could be roused from his sloth. If he *was* restored to the throne the rewards for me would be considerable. The role of 'number one idiot' to a reigning monarch was an enviable one. I would live in great style in the palace in a luxurious apartment, enjoy the best food and wine and was sure to be given valuable presents when I particularly amused my master – clothes, jewels, even possibly grants of land. In addition I would be a powerful figure in my own right and for my entertainment would be able to make free use of any young servant girl or boy according to my taste.

On the night before a battle, there is always a lot of activity, and noise, in the camp. It was a warm August evening, so I decided to sleep in the open. I walked away from all the bustle into the darkened and peaceful countryside. I found myself a sheltered patch of ground at the edge of a wood and rolled myself up in a blanket I had brought with me. I slept fairly well and was hardly troubled by a rain shower in the early hours. At first light, I awoke, rather stiff, stretched, rolled up my blanket and made my way back.

The rain had passed and the morning was fine. To an outsider, the scene would look to be one of total chaos and they wouldn't be far wrong. Knights, already in armour, were checking their weaponry and supervising the grooming of their horses. Archers were sharpening their arrows and testing the strength of their bows. The infantry, most of them, were leaning sullenly on their pikes. Some people might attempt to get a scrap of breakfast, though few had any appetite and everywhere men could be seen shouting and gesticulating even though nobody appeared to be paying the slightest attention to them. But all this had nothing to do with me. My place was with the baggage train, where I would wait in relative safety for the outcome of the battle. I did notice, though that the camp seemed to be smaller than I remembered it from the previous afternoon. Perhaps some of the weaker spirits had slunk away under cover of darkness. If they had, I wouldn't be surprised.

I felt rough arms clasp me from behind. "I've been looking for you." I turned round and found myself looking into an ugly pock-marked face. I recognised it as belonging to one of thugs who 'protected' the 'good old king'.

"You are coming with me." The man's breath stank of ale and I caught the full force. He began to shove me forward and, as he was at least twice my size I was in no position to resist.

"What does he want?" I asked. Surely our leader didn't expect me to stand around making wisecracks while he prepared for battle. Even he must realise that this was a solemn moment for any man.

"Never you mind," my escort replied and gave me another none too gentle shove. We made our way across the camp until we came to a large tent. I had never been inside but I knew what it was – the armourer's tent.

My new-found friend gave me one final shove which propelled me through the door and almost knocked me off my feet.

"Here he is."

"Skinny little runt, isn't he. Hardly bigger than a boy." The voice belonged to a well-built middle-aged individual who had exceptionally strong forearms and calloused rough hands. "We won't find anything to fit him."

"Oh yes we will." The speaker was the biggest man I have ever seen, well over six and a half feet tall and muscled in proportion. He looked like a brainless bruiser, the sort who would be employed to keep order in a rowdy tavern. I knew he was nothing of the kind. He *was* immensely strong but he was also a respected and highly-skilled craftsman. He was the armourer.

"He is about Lord Richard's size."

Lord Richard *was* a boy, just 16 years old but already a courageous and proven warrior. He was the son of the Earl of Huntingdon whose forces were due to join up with the 'good old king' before the battle. His arrival was expected any minute.

"But Lord Richard will be needing his armour today."

"Lord Richard might well be needing his armour today. But as his father has changed sides and his soldiers will be fighting for the enemy rather than us, Lord Richard can ride into battle naked for all I care."

"Come on you." The armourer quickly stripped off my motley and reached for a coat of chain mail which he started to place over my head.

"You've got it all wrong," I protested. "I'm not a warrior. I don't fight, I'm a fool. The king's jester."

"Everyone fights today. No exceptions. The king's orders. Even the chefs are going into battle. I don't know what they are expected to do. Hit the opposing soldiers over the head with a frying pan I suppose – though personally I think our chefs would do more damage to the enemy troops if they cooked their meals for them."

"You don't understand," I cried out desperately. "I don't fight. I'm a fool. Do you hear me? I'm a fool. I'm a fool."

The armourer looked out of the tent. About a mile away at the top of a slight incline were the enemy. There seemed to be thousands of them – knights, bowmen, foot-soldiers. All lined up in battle-order. There was open ground between our army and theirs, but woods were on either side. It was easy to see how, when they attacked, our forces could be trapped and the open ground turned into a bloody killing field.

The armourer surveyed the scene for a couple of minutes, then he turned back into the tent.

"We're all fools today," he said quietly.

Sergeant Leopard

Rawsewage-on-sea has a decaying pier, a stony beach, two overpriced luxury hotels, a score of down-at-heel guest houses, crazy golf, fish and chip shops, greasy-spoon cafes, three pretentious gastropubs, a rusting Ferris wheel, a litter-strewn promenade and a biting east wind which blows on 350 days a year – in fact, a typical British seaside resort.

Recently, though, the crime rate had been soaring; stores had been robbed, beach huts broken into, innocent citizens mugged and OAPs beaten up.

The Important People of the town held a meeting. "This has got to stop!" said the mayor. The borough treasurer agreed as did the president of the chamber of commerce and the secretary of the mothers' union.

"But what is to be done?" asked the mayor after two-and-a-half hours of ineffectual blathering. They all looked at each other, and then chanted in unison.

"SEND FOR SERGEANT LEOPARD."

So they did.

The sergeant prowled in to town at night, so as not to attract attention. With an experienced eye, he surveyed the scene then climbed up an ash tree, not far from a cash machine. He was well hidden with leaves even covering the stripes on his sleeve. He had to wait – but then he was good at waiting. For three days nothing significant happened.

Then an old lady went up to the machine. Two youths in leather jackets stood menacingly behind her. The lady put her bank card into the machine.

One of the yobs approached her.

"OK, Gran. We know you are loaded. Give us yer pin number or it'll be the worse for you."

He grabbed the old lady's arm and began to twist it behind her back.

The old lady wasn't sure what happened next. There was a growl, a blur of yellow and black, some terrified screams and the sound of munching and crunching. Suddenly the youths were no longer bothering her but their mangled bodies were lying in the road in two bleeding heaps. Taking care not to slip in the gore and slime the old lady withdrew her cash from the machine and gratefully made her way home.

A week later, Sergeant Leopard foiled an armed hold-up at a betting shop. He efficiently disabled the gunman (who in future would be known as a 'one-arm bandit') and prevented the escape of his accomplice (who in future would be known as a 'one-leg bandit').

Sergeant Leopard then set off in pursuit of the getaway car. Although the driver accelerated as fast as he could he never stood a chance. In a few swift strides Sergeant Leopard caught up with the vehicle. He received a commendation from the chief constable for the way he leapt onto the roof, smashed open a side window then bent down and bit off the driver's head.

An important football match was about to take place in the town. As there had been a lot of trouble in the past it was proposed to send in extra police but the mayor said that reinforcements wouldn't be necessary. And they weren't.

The away team supporters passed the time before the match in their usual fashion: smashing-up pubs, looting shops, kicking old age pensioners, vomiting in drinking fountains and beating to a pulp anyone wearing a Rawsewage Rovers scarf.

Sergeant Leopard caught up with them in the pleasure gardens. After he had spent fifteen minutes dispensing his unique brand of justice, the state of the park resembled the aftermath of the Battle of Agincourt. As one local undertaker said "I have been in this business for thirty years and it's the first time I have had to hire a JCB to scrape up human remains."

Word soon spread about Sergeant Leopard and potential lawbreakers steered clear of Rawsewage-on-sea. The town became virtually crime-free and extremely prosperous. All was well.

Sergeant Leopard was not happy, though. He tried his best to be a conscientious police officer but he was not cut out for filling-in forms, helping old ladies across the road and trying to find stolen bicycles. As a result he became bored and tended to react aggressively to quite trivial incidents. When he was walking the beat one night he was approached by a harmless drunk who patted him on the head and said "You're not a real leopard."

Was it necessary to chew off the poor man's arm as far as the elbow? Especially when the sergeant had scoffed a large portion of egg and chips in the police canteen only an hour before.

One day a passenger came in to complain about the late running of the municipal buses. The sergeant prowled round to the company's offices to 'sort out the problem'. After his visit all that could be found on the premises was a half-eaten bus conductor's half-eaten hat.

A resident of Sunset Villas – expensive homes on the cliff-top – phoned to report that he was being burgled. Sergeant Leopard responded to the call and tossed the house-breaker so high in the air that when he landed in the sea the splash could be heard in Dieppe.

Sergeant Leopard's fate was finally sealed when, one summer's day, a rather plump and flustered young lady came into the police station.

"It's a disgrace!" she complained. "All these grockles, packing out the beach. There's no room for us locals. Where am I supposed to take the kids?"

"Leave this to me madam," said Sergeant Leopard and strode purposefully out of the door. He went down to the beach and set to work with a will.

By the time he had finished, there was so much blood on the shingle and so many mutilated corpses floating in the water that you would think they had just finished filming a particularly gruesome scene from *Jaws*.

Unfortunately, the incident made the front page of the *Daily Express* and got a mention on *News at Ten*. Tourists stopped coming and as the town's livelihood was dependent on visitors this was a disaster for Rawsewage-on-sea.

The police authority (chairman – his worship the mayor) issued Sergeant Leopard with a Naughty Carnivore Summons. The sergeant realised that his career was on the line and as a conscientious officer, he was very depressed.

Yes, it was a sad leopard that appeared before the Disciplinary Committee and a sad leopard that ate them.

Guessing that he was in real trouble, Sergeant Leopard raced along the promenade in leaps and bounds then sped up the hill and out of town.

Gradually, Rawsewage-on-sea returned to normal. The tourists came back and so did the bad guys – leaving the local police to enforce the law as best they could.

Some people yearned for 'The Good Old Days' when Sergeant Leopard kept the place virtually crime-free but most thought that if having a 'totally-safe' town meant also having a 'totally-empty' town, the price was too high.

But once a copper, always a copper. Sergeant Leopard removed the stripes from his sleeve – the worst moment of his life but it had to be done. In another town, not far from here, ex-Sergeant Leopard is, even now, in a recruitment office filling in an application form.

He is confident he will be taken on. Though some might question his methods, he knows that there will always be a place in the force for an officer with his exceptional abilities. He studies police law in the evenings and he keeps his claws sharp.

Groucho had to throw his elder brother out of the family comedy act. Karl had absolutely no sense of humour.

Dialogue between Two Lords of Creation

CREATOR A   It's very quiet.
CREATOR B   I know. That's because nothing has happened yet.
CREATOR A   Nothing?
CREATOR B   No, nothing. The universe hasn't started to form.
CREATOR A   So how will we know when it *does* start?
CREATOR B   That's easy. There will be a *Big Bang*.
CREATOR A   What's a *Big Bang*?
CREATOR B   A noise.
CREATOR A   A loud noise?
CREATOR B   Oh yes. A *very* loud noise.
CREATOR A   So, until this *Big Bang*, there's nothing. No matter exists at all?
CREATOR B   *(Humouring him)* That's right. Nothing at all.
CREATOR A   But sound can't travel through 'nothing' - through a vacuum. So how are we going to hear this loud noise? This *Big Bang*?
CREATOR B   *(Silence)*
CREATOR A   I said –
CREATOR B   I know what you said.
CREATOR A   So, what's your answer?
CREATOR B   *(Long pause)* I'll have to think about it.

                Enter CREATOR C

CREATOR C   *(Talking directly to the audience)* Okay guys, now you have seen these two, does anyone still believe in *Intelligent Design?*

Cool It, Dad

The sun was hot on his skin and it was very good just to lie on the grass and look at the sky. Much better than the darkness. The boy had been very frightened in the darkness.

And he had a girl lying beside him. Her flesh was warm to the touch and, as he leant over to kiss her, he was reminded of how good it was to be alive.

Yes, he had been frightened in the darkness, though he had tried not to show it. He had trusted his father when he said everything would be all right. His father was a very clever man, even if a tedious old windbag.

The lad looked up at the sun. Time to move.

"See you here? Same time tomorrow?" she asked.

"Sure," he replied. But he wouldn't be here tomorrow. He would be miles away.

When the boy reached the meeting-place, a clearing in the woods, surrounded by trees (secrecy was essential) his father was still working busily.

Where have you been?" he demanded angrily. "Oh never mind, I can guess. We're almost ready to go. Now listen carefully."

He closed his mind as Dad droned on. He had been through these instructions a million times. The boy knew them by heart. He just wanted to be off and away.

"Keep close to me and don't try anything silly. Understand?"

"Cool it, Dad. I know what I'm doing. Right?"

"You've never flown before, lad."

"Neither have you."

Dad took off first. At the start the boy did keep close by, but almost without realising, he went higher and higher. He could see the green of the island, the sandy beaches, the blue ocean and poor old Dad trundling along, way below, at zero feet. This was the life. No thoughts of the dark cave now. The boy shouted out loud, brimming over with excitement and joy. Nobody would ever catch them now. They were free at last.

He was soaring up like a bird but no bird had ever flown so high. Then he began to feel hot. That wasn't right. There must be something wrong. The boy glanced round and began to panic.

Sweating, he tried to regain control but to no avail. For an agonising moment, he was totally stationary – suspended motionless between earth and sky. Then he started to fall, slowly at first, but he rapidly gained speed, plunging helplessly towards the unforgiving ocean. He screamed for help at the top of his voice but his cries were carried away by the wind. The sea rushed up to meet him and Icarus knew one final moment of pure terror, before he crashed into the water with a resounding splash.

She wasn't surprised when the boy didn't turn up the next day. She had known he wouldn't. After all, she was only a simple country girl and he, what was he? She had asked him once.

"I'm an airline pilot."

"No, you aren't. You are far too young."

"All right, I am not actually an airline pilot but I'm training to be one. And I'm nineteen."

"Which company?"

"BOAC."

She didn't believe him, though she wanted to. And something about the way he spoke made her think that he was foreign. Spanish, maybe or Italian. And now things had ended as she always knew they would end. But though uneducated she was a girl of spirit so she went into the nearest BOAC offices.

"I'm afraid, miss, that is information I cannot divulge. The identities of our pilots are strictly confidential."

"But you can tell me at what age you take on trainees."

"Twenty-one."

Now she was glad she had at last, given in to Paul Thompson. That rather uncomfortable romp in the hayloft meant that she could plausibly claim the baby was his. And he was crazy about her. He had already asked her to marry him twice. And Paul wasn't a bad catch. His father owned a fair-sized farm which Paul would inherit one day. He was tall, strong, good-looking, hard-working and kind hearted. Could she really ask for more?

This was England in 1959 before the Lady Chatterley trial, before the Beatles, before the Swinging Sixties had began to untie the bonds of the British class system. People might have 'never had it so good' but everyone knew their place. As a labourer's daughter she would be taking a step up by marrying Paul. A level-headed young woman, she was content with her lot. In a way, she was glad that the boy had broken his promise and hadn't come back. She knew it would never work out. A girl such as her could never fall in love with a trainee airline pilot or a Greek God who flew too close to the sun.

Morning Routine

"These won't go very far." Muriel Smith looked disdainfully at the two rather scrawny mackerel.

"It was either them or cod fillets in batter," replied her husband. Dennis Smith sighed. Since he had retired he had developed a settled morning routine. Half an hour in the bookies, a couple of pints with his mates at the British Legion and then he would do the food shopping. Although Muriel said that she was pleased to 'get him out of the house' for a couple of hours, she found fault with whatever delights Dennis brought back from *Tesco Express* to their semi-detached bungalow in Weybridge.

But Dennis was now an experienced campaigner. Show her the worst first and let her have her moan.

"I have done better with the loaves," he said in a confident voice. "Two large brown, two soft white sliced and a granary."

Muriel sniffed. She was somewhat placated. But only somewhat. She changed the subject.

"From the sound of it, there are a lot of people outside."

"Yes, quite a crowd," agreed Dennis.

"How many, would you say?"

"I don't know. I didn't count them."

"You *should* know. You've been out there."

"Yes and you should know as well because you've been peeping through the lace curtains," thought Dennis. Aloud he said "At a guess, about five thousand."

Muriel looked concerned. "Oh dear, five thousand hungry people to feed and we've only got two fishes and five loaves. I hope it will be enough."

The Fish Market

The man in the long overcoat pulled his hat down over his ears. There was a chill early morning wind blowing and he felt out of place on the draughty quay. He was a scholar, an academic and had an uneasy sense that everyone was looking at him as he waited patiently in line. He could see that the woman in front had a full basket of what appeared to be herrings and he had only one fish to sell. But it was a fine fish. He remembered the advice Peter had given him, Peter who had grown up amongst these people.

"Don't be put off by his appearance. Bargain. Haggle. He'll be surprised but he will increase his offer."

When he reached the front of the queue, the man in the long overcoat *was* rather startled. But he kept his nerve, bargained and did get a better price.

As he walked away, the man in the long overcoat smiled, partly out of relief and partly because the person who had bought the fish had seemed comical rather than menacing, as if he was acting a part in a second-rate play. The beard and moustache were obviously stuck on, the horns were askew, the tail seemed to be a piece of old rope, the red body paint was already wearing off and the pitchfork leaning against the table was made out of cardboard.

"Still, I've done what I came to do," thought Dr Faustus. "I've sold my sole to the Devil."

Conversation Piece

The two young men looked out of place in the gentleman's club and not just because of their youth. Though it is true that most of the members were anything up to fifty years older and many were sitting in the comfortable leather armchairs in a state of such immobility that they could be mistaken for dead men. In fact quite a few probably *were* dead and would be discreetly removed later by the cleaning staff. These senior members were mostly military types and their conversation consisted of little more than accounts of how they had bested Lord Kitchener in an argument about strategy or reminiscences of pig-sticking in The Punjab, punctuated by a shout of "Bearer! Another chota peg!"

The two young men were out of place because they were discussing poetry.

"You must admit, Bill that, in the public's eyes you are *the* poet of the Lake District," said one young man who was dressed in a three-piece suit. He had neatly-parted dark hair, rather prominent ears and a precise manner of speech with a hint of a transatlantic accent.

"I hate the Lake District," said the other young man, who was wearing a dark coat with an exaggerated ruff at the neck. You might easily have taken him for a Regency dandy, an impression enhanced by his rather foppish manner. "The Lake District is remote, isolated, it rains all the time, the people are uncouth and ignorant and how sick I get of the scenery. Scenery my foot, all those sodden mountains and windswept stretches of grey water. How anyone can see any beauty in the God forsaken county of Westmorland is beyond me. The whole place is just a wasteland, Tom. And, what is more, I loathe living in the eighteenth century."

"Hey, wait a minute, Bill you wrote *Bliss was it in that dawn to be alive. But to be young was very heaven.* Remember?"

"I dare say I did, Tom. I've written reams of twaddle in my time. You can't expect me to remember all of it. You really have no idea what the eighteenth century is like. No electric light, no decent plumbing, the whole place looks so shabby. We are never really warm and, if I do venture out, I have to climb on some useless spindly nag who, when I'm already soaked to the skin will like as not tip me into a ditch. Why here in London in – what is it – 1922? you have convenient means of transport, central heating and a high level of comfort. I mean, Tom, have you ever *sat* on a Chippendale chair? Why, if I could live in London in 1922, what with buses, tubes and taxis I reckon I could stay warm and dry all winter, I wouldn't really have to go outdoors at all."

"We can't choose our time and place, you know that, Bill. We have to make the best of what we are given. By the way, do you have anything for me?"

The other man looked even more gloomy, if that was possible. "Only one line and I am afraid that is not very good."

"Let me have a look. Ah yes, I see what you mean. *I wandered lonely as a cloud.* Not very accurate is it? Not in this country, Bill. Clouds are never lonely. In fact, they have a remarkable herding instinct and congregate together to form a huge blanket which covers the land for days, even weeks, on end. Now, if you were to write *lonely as a ray of sunshine* or *lonely as a patch of blue sky* that would make more sense. Anyway, I will see what I can do with it."

The smart young man in the three-piece suit wrote for a few moments and then handed the paper to his companion who read what had been written and then let out a cry of horror.

"Oh no. It's all about daffodils. I detest daffodils, Tom. You can't imagine how awful the daffodil season is. The whole place is covered with the sodding things and the countryside turns a revolting bilious yellow. Honestly, just to look at them makes me feel physically sick. For a couple of months when the daffodils are flowering I stay indoors with the blinds drawn. I daren't even peep out of the window without getting a headache."

"Well, I have only done the first verse, Bill and you are welcome to it. I can't use it. My public won't accept stuff like that."

The dandified young man shook his head. "What about you, Tom?" His companion handed him a smart leather-bound notebook. "Hey, you can't say that!"

"Can't say what, Bill?"

"*April is the cruellest month.* That's just as bad as *I wandered lonely as a cloud*. April is *not* the cruellest month. April signifies the end of the God awful depressing winter and the coming of what we ironically call 'summer'. I know the weather never really gets warm and the rain continues unabated but there *are* one or two days when one is able to venture outside for an hour or two without actually catching pneumonia. No, Tom, if there is a month in the Lake District when one might feel some sort of hope that things could improve, that month is April."

"Sure, I know that. But I have to consider my reputation. Everything I write has to be demonstrably untrue or completely meaningless. If I was ever to produce anything comprehensible I would be finished as a poet."

Bill rose from the leather armchair with a sigh. "I suppose, I had better be getting back to the Lake District – and the eighteenth century."

"Aren't you forgetting one thing?" asked Tom.

Bill looked puzzled.

"My pen. You still have my pen. You can't take a fountain pen back to the eighteenth century."

"Damn. I thought you hadn't noticed. You don't know what a pain in the arse it is writing with a quill. All those splodges and blots and you have to stop to sharpen the fucking thing every few minutes."

The other man said nothing but held out his hand. Reluctantly Bill gave him the pen then stomped out of the room muttering.

Tom opened his leather notebook, thought for a few moments and then wrote a couple of lines and smiled.

"That should keep the English Departments of several universities guessing for years, even decades. I reckon these lines will spawn a dozen PhDs and at least three books and still no-one will be able to figure out what they mean because of course they are complete gibberish but, even though I say so myself very profound gibberish."

Tom chuckled as he re-read what he had written.
*"Garlic and sapphires in the mud
Clog the bedded axle-tree."*

The Astronomer (Part Two)

A week later, after their initial interrogation of the Astronomer, Cardinals Enchilada and Wolsey were seated in the same room, belching contentedly.

"Shall we start?" asked Enchilada.

"Where is Cardinal Dracula?" asked Wolsey.

"Oh, it's after dark. He is out searching for virgins."

"I used to work for a man who did the same thing."

"Yes, but he wanted to marry them, not bite their necks and suck their blood."

"Sometimes I think my life might have been a lot easier if Henry VIII *had* been a vampire," sighed Wolsey.

Enchilada turned and spoke to a fat man who was standing nearby. He had a pointed nose, grey hair and a tendency to suddenly start grinning inanely and bursting into shoulder-shaking laughter.

"Heath, bring in the prisoner. Wait a minute, though. Who is that effete looking young man leaning against the wall?"

"He's a Lollard, Your Eminence," replied Heath.

"You were supposed to have burnt all the Lollards months ago. Get a grip, Heath or I'll have you replaced. Never mind. Bring in the prisoner anyway."

The Astronomer was thinner and paler after a week in the stinking rat-infested cell – a week spent confronting his own demons (the Devil had been too busy to pay him a visit). Though the Astronomer was frightened, more than that, he was terrified – he was determined not to confess. "They have no proof," he kept saying to himself. "Remember, they have no proof."

"Have you come to your senses?" asked Cardinal Enchilada in his usual hectoring manner.

"I am merely a simple scholar who notes what he observes. I make no -"

"Oh God, don't give me all that again. Perhaps this will make you change your mind." The cardinal picked up a leather-bound volume which was lying on the desk in front of him and showed it to the Astronomer.

"Well?"

"It's my notebook," said the scientist. "How did you get hold of it?"

"My agents raided your study and seized it."

"On what authority?"

"On the authority vested in the Inquisition by the Holy Church to root out and destroy heresy," replied Cardinal Enchilada. "Anyway, it is just as well for you that the book was seized because, soon afterwards, a violent mob, drunk on cheap wine and well-paid from the pontifical coffers, set fire to your house in disgust at the prospect of an Albigensian living in the same street. Their murderous rage was in no way lessened by the fact that they had no idea who Albert Jensen was."

"I'm not an Alb -"

"Be quiet. Now I'm no scholar – in fact, I can hardly read and write but that hasn't hindered my ecclesiastical career. However, your notebook has been shown to distinguished experts and they are of the unanimous opinion that your observations point to one conclusion. Can you guess what it is?"

"That the Earth moves round the Sun," replied the Astronomer.

"Exactly," agreed Cardinal Enchilada. "This slim volume, illegally filched from private property, provides conclusive evidence that you are a dangerous heretic, an instrument of Satan working to undermine the lawful authority of the Legitimate Church. And you know what happens to heretics."

The Astronomer prostrated himself on the floor.

"I confess, Your Eminence, that my records as set down in my notebooks do seem to support the proposition that the Earth orbits the Sun. But these records are inaccurate. I deliberately falsified them in order to gain fame and worldly glory. I was, indeed, led astray by the Devil. I know that the Earth is the centre of the Universe, that it is fixed in the firmament and remains stationary while the sun, moon and stars revolve around it. Oh, most gracious Cardinal Enchilada, show me mercy, I beg of you, I have seen the error of my ways. I'll be a good boy in future, I will never claim that the Earth moves. Spare me please. I don't want to be burnt."

"Oh for Christ's sake, get him out of here before I throw up," said Cardinal Enchilada. "If there's one thing that turns my stomach, it is a repentant sinner, grovelling on the floor, pleading for forgiveness."

Heath yanked the gibbering Astronomer to his feet. Enchilada looked at him with loathing and disgust.

"The Earth remains fixed in space. Have you got that fact into your thick skull?"

"Yes, Your Eminence." But as he was led out of the room the Astronomer turned and spoke again. "And yet it -"

"Naughty, naughty," cut in Enchilada. "Don't try and steal the scene. That's not your line and you know it."

"So what do we do now?" asked Cardinal Wolsey, when the two prelates were once more alone.

"We will leave the wretched fellow in the stinking, rat-infested cell for a month or two, wallowing in his own excrement, and then release him," replied Cardinal Enchilada.

"Release him?"

"Oh yes."

"And his book? I suppose that will be burnt."

"No, we are going to publish it."

"Publish it?" Wolsey was horrified.

"Let me explain." Enchilada raised his voice. "Heath, bring in the monk who is outside, wanking in the corridor."

A rather sheepish-looking friar entered, hastily tying the rope that circled his ample waist and wiping his hands on his cloak.

"That's a filthy habit," said Enchilada.

"I know," replied the monk. "But the laundry is so busy, these days. They spend all their time washing blood-stained clothing from the torture chambers."

"Are you certain that you have done your work well, Thelonious?" asked Enchilada.

"Yes, Your Eminence," replied the monk. "Though I say so myself, I have accomplished a very clever piece of counterfeiting. When the book is first published it will cause a sensation and revolutionise the way scholars regard the universe. But within, say six months, some clever-dick will find that the work, though superficially convincing does, in fact, contain many serious mistakes. Then the Astronomer's findings will be entirely discredited."

When the monk had left the room, Enchilada spoke again.

"You see the scheme which I so brilliantly have formulated,

my dear Wolsey. The volume we have in front of us is *not* the Astronomer's journal but a skilful forgery, created by the monk and it is this fake that we are going to present to the world. As Thelonious rightly remarked, when the calculations are found to be strewn with errors the conclusion of the work, namely that the Earth moves round the Sun, will be shown to be a fallacy and the Astronomer, far from being acclaimed as a great scientist, will be exposed as a cheat and a fraudster. And the best part is, that the Astronomer won't be able to defend himself against such allegations because all his papers were destroyed in the fire."

"But that doesn't solve the problem," objected Cardinal Wolsey. "We are both aware that the Astronomer is right – the Earth *does* move round the Sun. Eventually some other scholar will compile enough evidence to prove this. What will you do then? Come up with another cunning plan? At the most you have bought some time – about fifty years I would guess."

"Who cares?" said Enchilada. "In fifty years we will all be dead."

"But think of the damage the truth, when it does come out, will do to the Church. You will have that on your conscience. Aren't you worried about your Immortal Soul?"

"I don't have an Immortal Soul," said Cardinal Enchilada. "And neither do you Wolsey. All this mumbo-jumbo we mouth, the fine robes we wear, the extravagant rituals we act out, it's merely a show put on for the benefit of children and the unwashed peasants – to stop them thinking for themselves. You know, as well as I do that there hasn't been a pontiff in the last three centuries who actually believed in the Resurrection.

Why does the Church waste so much of its hard-earned cash on alms for the poor if it really is possible to feed 5000 people on a couple of herrings and five loaves of bread? And when did you last see a dead beggar take up his bed and walk? The last one I kicked certainly didn't.

Look around you at the state of the world, all the wars that are being waged and bloody battles fought in the name of God. *Blesséd are the peacemakers?* I don't think so. And *are* the meek going to inherit the earth? Not if I can help it they aren't."

"Are you saying that God is dead?"

"No, I'm not saying God is dead. I'm saying he never existed," replied Cardinal Enchilada. "Look, would you have led the kind of self-centred and avaricious life you did or committed the brutal crimes that you have, if you thought that one day, you would be called to account and would have to justify your actions in front of a Supreme Being? I know I wouldn't.

If there was a God, wouldn't He have endowed us with a conscience, given us a sense of right and wrong? And neither you nor I would recognise a moral scruple if it jumped up and bit us in the face, would we?"

"If that is what you believe, why did you join the Church?" asked Wolsey.

"Because I love dressing-up and I rather fancy being pope. I could have a lot of fun excommunicating my many enemies."

"Are you sure you will become pope?" asked Wolsey.

"Oh yes," replied Enchilada confidently. "If the conclave is being difficult and it doesn't appear that the election is going my way, I will have to make use of the skills I learnt in my previous employment."

"And what was your previous employment?"

"I was a poisoner. You see I am not really called 'Enchilada'. That is only a *nom d'église*. I was born a Borgia and despite the onerous nature of my ecclesiastical duties, I still take a great interest in the family business. In fact, I'm just off to take a glass of wine with my cousin Lucretia. Would you care to join us?"

"I wouldn't have sex with you if you were
the only man on the planet."
"Tough shit, Eve."

Slave Labour

It was still dark when, half asleep, we started to assemble. There must have been thousands of us. I have never seen so many slaves in the same place. This was clearly a huge project.

I don't remember much about the countryside – it was rather hilly and I think there was a river. Yes, I'm sure there was a river, a large river.

As we began to line up in front of the gangmaster, I kept well-back, nicely hidden. It's a good idea not to get noticed when you are a slave. That's how I survived for so long, by not being noticed.

One of the Macedonians at the front, shouted up to the gangmaster,

"What are we doing today, boss?"

A chippy lot the Macedonians – the wise guys of the Ancient World.

"We are going to build a city."

"Does it have a name, this city we are going to build?"

"Rome."

"Rome wasn't built in a day!" shouted another Macedonian.

That wasn't clever. Two of the gangmaster's bodyguards grabbed the unfortunate wretch by the arms while a third bodyguard slipped a rope over his neck.

Quicker than it takes to tell, the mouthy Macedonian was hanging from a branch of a tree, choking his life away.

The rest of us got the message.

"Why do I always get the blame?" asked the scapegoat.
"Because it is always your fault."

St George

I began that day as an ordinary knight in shining armour, idly trotting through the countryside on my trusty milk white steed. My mind was distracted from its customary noble thoughts by the sound of yelling and shouting. Looking up, I saw a group of people on the walls of a nearby fortified town – they were gesticulating and pointing at me.

I thought about making a suitable gesture in return but instead headed for the town gate which was opened to let me in. I was soon surrounded by the usual crowd of gawping half-wits, brain-damaged beggars and drooling village idiots. A little fat man who was wearing a red tunic and sweating profusely spoke.

"Are you a knight in shining armour?" he asked.

I felt like saying that I was really Friar Tuck in disguise but the townsfolk were so agitated, that I didn't think it was time for frivolity.

"You must help us," the little fat man continued. "One of our princesses has been kidnapped," he wailed. "She was taken in the middle of the night by a fire-breathing monster."

I stifled a yawn. Not that old story.

Really, under the rules of chivalry, I had little choice. So, brandishing my sword fiercely and looking as warlike as possible for someone with a humongous hangover, I galloped impressively out of the town in pursuit of the dragon.

It was easy to pick up his trail by following scorch marks on the grass; and after about half-an-hour, I came upon the monster standing outside his cave breathing flames and snorting defiance. The girl lay in a heap on the ground. With any luck I would be too late and if that was so, I could honourably return to the town without having to fight the beast.

I dismounted and went over to the princess. I touched her face. It was still warm. I felt her pulse. Dammit, the stupid cow was still alive. The monster gave another snort and glared at me malevolently. Clearly he didn't think I was going to be much of an opponent.

Now it was all over and the dragon was lying dead at my feet, he looked so much smaller. He was no longer a threat – his tail twitching and his nostrils gently smouldering. It was not yet midday but (although I didn't know it) I was already a hero for all time.

The townsfolk were delighted that I had rescued their damsel in distress and cheered so loudly that the stench of foul breath almost made me pass out.

The fat little man was particularly overjoyed – it turned out that the girl I had rescued was his daughter.

"Oh brave sir, won't you stay and marry the princess?"

I must say I was tempted, because then I could look forward to an existence of luxury and ease living in a big castle. Okay, so the town was a putrid, unhygienic, plague-ridden, rat-infested, shit-hole. But everywhere is the same these days. That's the Middle Ages for you.

I was just about to reply to the offer of his daughter's hand (and I hope the rest of her) in marriage, when my hypersensitive ears heard a 'chink' sound. I noticed a small sack being passed round the crowd, into which grateful citizens were dropping gold coins. That put a different complexion on the matter.

I tried (not very successfully) to look modest then I explained to the townsfolk that I had 'urgent feudal duties to perform' and told them that I was 'already late for the Third Crusade'. As soon as the fat freak had presented me with the bag of swag, I galloped off into the gathering dusk.

As I rode away, I turned my mind to the strange events of the morning. I had been standing over the princess, wondering how soon I could make my excuses and leave. Suddenly, the dragon charged at me, a ten-foot long jet of flame spurting forth from his mouth. I tried to turn and run but sheer terror kept me rooted to the spot. I closed my eyes and, in a seemingly-futile gesture of resistance, aimed my sword at the fearsome beast. The dragon leapt at me, and I felt the searing heat of his fiery breath. The point of my blade scarcely scratched his scaly skin but immediately the monster collapsed in a heap at my feet. Dead. I was amazed. Some sort of miracle, I guess.

Don't get me wrong. Deserved or not, I intend to fully exploit my newly-won fame. I mean, who wouldn't want to be a patron saint? But I take good care to ensure my reward cash is safely stashed away. After all, no-one can live on glory forever.

Before the Fall

I was walking home, taking a shortcut across the fields on a fine September afternoon. White cumulus clouds, tinged with a little grey, were floating in a blue sky. One cloud, in particular, caught my attention because it was shaped exactly like an alpine mountain – complete with summit and also ridges, crests and gullies. It was a remarkable coincidence, even rather uncanny.

As I watched, I saw what looked like a small human figure who seemed to be climbing one of the ridges. Fortunately, I still had my binoculars with me; they were a military issue and spying, for me has, regrettably, become second nature.

I was soon able to focus on the cloud and found that my first impression had, indeed, been correct. I watched, fascinated, as he made his way carefully up the ridge, selecting hand and footholds and occasionally chipping away with his ice-axe. In fact, I was so engrossed that I failed to notice that the mountain was fast dissolving – the cloud was being eaten away from the inside, so that soon only a sliver remained, completely surrounded by blue sky. And then, even that slice had gone and the man was suspended in mid-air.

I knew what was going to happen next. So, I think, did the climber, for he seemed to glance down as if aware of his predicament. I did not wish to witness the unlucky individual's fall and messy death so I lowered my binoculars and turned away.

In addition, as the activities I had been engaged in that afternoon were undoubtedly illegal, I did not want to be discovered by the authorities.

There was no mention of the incident on the late-night TV news but, next day, the unfortunate man made the headlines in all the morning papers.

Merton and Callum

Merton and Callum, two young biologists, were getting drunk in the *White Hart*.

"It's Frankenstein's fault," said Merton. "People are afraid to create a 'monster'. That was 200 years ago. Now, we have the technology."

"Then let's do it," urged Callum.

They tossed a coin. Callum won so he chose to be the monster. Merton decided to turn Callum into the sort of green Venusian he'd seen in his dad's old Dan Dare annuals.

When the transformation was complete, Merton took Callum to a Halloween party. He was a great success. The next morning, Merton woke with a bad hangover. Groaning, he staggered into his laboratory. Callum had escaped and had also taken the remote which controlled all his actions.

Merton wasn't worried. There was a spare remote control locked in a safe, which Callum didn't know about.

That was gone as well.

"Bad news. He's more intelligent than I planned."

As Callum was almost indestructible and had a grudge against the world, he would be able to cause immense havoc. It would probably take a tactical nuclear missile to demolish him.

"Best get far away," thought Merton as he booked himself on the next flight to New Zealand.

Midnight Train

"I am not going, I really am not." Rhoda Lewis had first heard the rumours at lunch time in the bank where she worked in a small mid-western town. She looked at herself in the dressing-table mirror. She was still only twenty-six with a rather elfin-shaped face, dark-brown hair, a snub-nose and what used to be described as 'dancing eyes'. Only those eyes hadn't danced much in the last two years – since the telegram arrived announcing that Ron was 'missing in action'.

It had been a fine July morning, still refreshingly cool but with the certainty of scorching heat to come when she had seen the telegraph boy walking up the drive. A scene she had played over in her mind a thousand times before. Not that she would claim to have experienced any sort of premonition but as a sensible girl she knew the score. Men who went away to war were often killed and there was no reason why it wouldn't happen to Ron. So as soon as the telegraph boy opened the gate, she acted out the events that followed as though she were in a familiar movie. She felt no emotion as she opened the envelope. She didn't even read the words.

Emotions would happen later. The sharp pang of jealousy as she saw a laughing young couple strolling in the park. Waking from a vivid dream, so heartbreakingly real and drowsily reaching out for Ron, followed by the horrible realisation as her hand touched nothing. The endless nights in her cold bed staring at the ceiling longing for sleep that would not come until the soft light of dawn stole into the room. The moments at work when she would burst into tears for no apparent reason and have to dash for the safety of the Ladies. And always, at the pit of her stomach, the continuous dull ache that would not go away.

Only when her mother saw the telegram did Rhoda realise that Ron was MIA rather than KIA. 'Missing in action' rather than 'killed in action'. Somewhere in Normandy. The name of the place meant nothing to Rhoda.

He might technically have been 'missing in action' but deep down Rhoda knew he wasn't. Some instinct told her that she would never see her husband again. And when the war ended and the prison camps had been liberated and there was still no sign of Ron, that hope faded entirely.

The telegram had arrived in July 1944. It was now September 1946.

"You ought to start getting your life together, seeing folks, maybe even start dating again."

Her mother, a widow, was an extremely practical person. Rhoda knew she was right. After all, before he had been sent to Europe, she had known Ron for a mere eighteen months. They had been married for twelve of those months and lived together as husband and wife for six. Rhoda knew she ought to 'draw a line' and 'move on' but the clichés proved much harder to fulfil than she had imagined. She knew intellectually that Ron was dead but somehow she was unable to accept the fact. Ridiculous though it was, she thought he would walk through the door at any moment. In a way, a very important way, she felt only half alive.

Marlene, at lunchtime, had made the first mention.

"Didya hear about the 'midnight train'?"

Marlene was a very slow-thinking person but was an accomplished stenographer and the fastest copy typist in the office. Vern her husband was an even slower-thinking person who had not only survived the war but was a decorated hero – a recipient of the Silver Star. It just wasn't fair. Rhoda felt the anger rise in her, then took a deep breath and calmed down.

"What midnight train, Marlene?"

"They say there's a train comin' in at midnight with released prisoners o'war and I thought that with your Ron still missin' an' all – he might be on it."

"There is no midnight train, Marlene. If Ron had been found, I would have been notified."

"Yeah, well, you know the army. The letter mighta got lost or sent to the wrong address."

There had been a great deal of talk in the office about the midnight train and several work colleagues, like Marlene, had suggested to Rhoda that she might go down to the station. When she arrived home, her mother had not been silent on the subject.

"No, Mom. I am not going to the station. There is no midnight train. Some rumour has got about causing an outbreak of mass hysteria. Have you ever read James Thurber's story 'The Day the Dam Broke'? Where one man running because 'he was late to meet his wife' causes a stampede in Columbus Ohio with everyone yelling 'Go East, the dam has broken'. Of course the dam hadn't broke. This rumour is just like that, an outbreak of mass hysteria." Then she added in a quiet voice. "No, I'm not being fair. It isn't mass hysteria. Just ordinary, hard-working people desperate to believe their loved ones are still alive, clinging to any hope however unlikely – just as I'm desperate to believe that Ron is still alive although I know he isn't."

Rhoda's mother went out to a friend's house to play bridge. The four 'old ladies' (they were in their mid-fifties) often became so engrossed in their game that it would be well after eleven before she got home. Rhoda deliberately didn't listen to the radio in case there was any mention of the 'midnight train'. She tried to read but gave up – the words weren't sinking in. She tried to do some knitting, then she listened to a gramophone record, then she played solitaire, then went back to reading again. But she just couldn't concentrate.

At half-past ten, when she would normally be thinking of retiring to bed she was far too keyed up to sleep. There was nothing for it. She simply must go to the station which was only about ten minutes' walk away.

When she arrived, there was already quite a crowd gathered. She estimated about a hundred people – mostly young women like her or middle-aged couples. Wives, sweethearts, parents. Although they were all waiting very patiently, some chatting quietly, Rhoda could feel the tension. Standing in a doorway, unobtrusive but keeping a watchful eye on proceedings was a well-built, silver-haired man in police uniform. She went up to him.

"Good evening, Uncle Jim," she said. "It looks like quite a gathering."

James McConnell was not Rhoda's uncle, though she had

known him since she was a child and always called him that. He was one of her father's oldest friends. They had been rookie cops together and been promoted up the ranks together, though Rhoda's father had always been promoted just that little bit ahead of Uncle Jim, who was now Chief of Police and, modestly, always said, "We all know that if your daddy was still around, he would be in this job, not me."

"Everything looks very peaceful," Rhoda remarked.

"The mayor's panicking as usual but I don't anticipate any trouble. When midnight comes and no train appears, folk will gradually start to drift away. I don't think there will be a stampede."

"So you don't believe there is going to be a train?"

"No, it's only a rumour."

Rhoda smiled. "But I bet you have made a plan just in case there is."

"I sure have. If you look around you can see there are half-a-dozen officers here but they are not to move unless I give the order." He looked at Rhoda sharply. "Do you believe there will be a train?"

"No, I don't."

"But you still had to come to the station?"

"Yes, I still had to come to the station."

Rhoda took a Lucky Strike cigarette from her bag and put it between her lips. Uncle Jim, ever the gentleman, offered her a light. As her father had died from lung cancer at the age of fifty-three, it might be thought strange that Rhoda still smoked. But in 1946, in America, nearly every adult smoked and no-one was aware of the link between cigarettes and the fatal disease.

As time went by, the conversations ceased and tension mounted. By ten minutes to twelve, the crowd was totally silent. It was a still night and a full moon was rising over the prairie – the sort of night where sounds travelled a long way. Suddenly, quite clearly was heard the 'WOOO' of a steam whistle in the distance. For a moment no-one in the crowd moved, then each turned to their neighbour and said "The Train" in a kind of awestruck whisper, still only half-believing.

A worried female voice called out, "How do we know the train is going to stop?"

There followed a harsh, rasping male voice, "It's gonna stop all right. We'll see to that."

People started to surge forward onto the tracks and for a moment, it looked as though there might be an ugly confrontation as the police officers on duty seemed to be holding back the crowd. This was not so. Uncle Jim had ordered that folk should be allowed onto the tracks as long as they advanced in a controlled manner and it was this that the cops were trying to achieve.

Uncle Jim had also given instructions that the signals in the station should be set at danger if the crowd moved on to the tracks. He checked to see that this had been done and then picked up a loud-hailer.

"Okay folks. You can now see the train is going to stop, so will you please stand back and leave the line clear?"

Jim was a popular and respected individual, so the throng gradually moved away to allow space for the train to pass. Then Jim himself climbed the steps up to the signal box. He didn't entirely trust Wes Clarkson. The signalman wouldn't allow a train to plough through a mass of people but now the line was clear he might just be tempted to 'change' the signal. Jim didn't blame Wes – after all, he was employed by the railroad company not the county. He thought he should be nice and close to prevent the signalman succumbing to temptation.

The train crept slowly into the station and then drew to a halt. There was an engine and six carriages. Again there was a surge as people were eager to climb on board. The cops were well prepared and made sure that those who wanted to enter the train did so in a disciplined fashion. Rhoda was not among them. She stood well back feeling almost ashamed. She now realised how stupid she had been, allowing herself to be swept away by the mass emotion. She was no better than Marlene. Calmer, Rhoda was able to assess the situation more rationally. Even assuming a letter from the army had 'gone astray', any return of prisoners wouldn't happen like this. There would be a properly organised official welcoming committee and it would happen at some civilised hour.

Not midnight. Rhoda was about to head home. If her mother had been particularly engrossed in her bridge game, Rhoda might make it back first and not have to admit to her foolishness.

Rhoda could see that the people who had first climbed on the train were descending with an air of disappointment.

But Rhoda did not go home.

For some reason she couldn't explain, she found herself walking towards the stationary train. Under police supervision, people had been allowed to get on at the sixth coach and walk right through to emerge from the first coach. Rhoda was the very last person to board and, as she filed along the carriages, she saw exactly what she expected to see. The only humans on board comprised the shuffling line of which she brought up the rear.

When they reached the end carriage, the line stopped moving. A railroad employee was addressing them. He was a slight, stooping, bespectacled man in his late forties. He seemed very bored as if he had recited the same words many times, as indeed he had.

"I tell you folks, contrary to any rumours you might have heard, there are no passengers on this train – as I guess you have seen for yourselves. This is not a scheduled service. These coaches are required at Topeka in the morning so we are running them up there. This is nothing unusual, it happens quite often. Now would you please disembark and allow us to proceed on our way."

The shuffle forward began again and everybody had alighted with the exception of Rhoda. Something made her turn round.

The coach was no longer empty.

Every seat was now occupied and in every seat was a young man in army uniform. But the uniforms were not neatly pressed as though about to go on parade. Most were torn, muddy or bloodstained. As for the men themselves, many bore obvious signs of having been in battle. Some had their arms in slings, some with huge bandages wrapped round their heads, others with legs encased in plaster. But this evidence of injury wasn't what Rhoda noticed about them. At this time of night, after a long journey, most of these soldiers would be sleeping, slumped in their seats, heads lolling. Others would be awake, quietly talking to their neighbour, lighting cigarettes, playing cards to while away the time or reading a newspaper or dime novel. It wasn't like that.

Each soldier was sitting bolt upright in his seat, his back ramrod-straight. Each was staring straight ahead with a fixed gaze. Rhoda suspected that their eyes, though wide-open were unseeing and every man's face was a ghostly, chalky white as if made-up to resemble some hideous parody of a circus clown.

Rhoda stared for a few moments. Then she saw him – about half-way down the coach. She showed no signs of recognition at first because she had never known him like this. She remembered a warm loving smile, a mirthful laugh, a look of wry amusement, a frown of concentration, even a burst of sudden anger, always short-lived. But never this rigid set expression as though he was an infernal waxwork sculpted by the Devil's hands.

"Ron," she shouted and started to run towards him. "Ron."

Then she felt strong hands grab her.

"Ron," she screamed.

Those hands, strong but surprisingly gentle, spun her round and she found herself looking into the face of the train guard.

"No, lady."

"But my husband –"

"No," he said again. Rhoda looked into the man's eyes. They were not the eyes of a tired railroad worker coming to the end of a difficult shift. In those eyes Rhoda saw wisdom, compassion, kindness. He not only understood the grief and anguish that Rhoda was experiencing, he was suffering with her.

"You can't go back. You know that."

Rhoda ceased to struggle, the tension went out of her body. For the first time in over two years she felt a kind of peace.

"Yes, I know that," she said quietly.

The man released his grip. Rhoda climbed down from the carriage. She stood with her head bowed as the engine blew its whistle and began to move off, resuming its interrupted journey.

"I will not look up, I will not look up," she vowed.

But, of course, she did look up. And as the train passed slowly by only a few feet from her, she could clearly see that every coach was entirely empty.

Night Patrol

The wind was howling through the trees. The rain was coming down harder and I was already soaked to the skin. Then my horse, a candidate for the knacker's yard, showing surprising energy, reared up and tipped me into a ditch. My friends think scaring people must be a great job but, believe me, on nights like these, life as a headless horseman is no joke.

At the end of my shift, just as dawn was breaking, the rain stopped and the sun came out. "Fucking typical," I thought. When I reached home, I saw that a dagger, grasped by a hand which was severed at the wrist and dripping blood, was sticking into my front door. Beneath the dagger was a note. (The post was early for once.) I was ordered to report to company headquarters, *Bram Stoker House*.

Charm school graduate, Maisie was, as usual, on duty and, as usual, she was smoking a cigarette.

"Oh, it's you. Go straight on up."

"What does he want?" I asked.

"I don't bleedin' know," she wheezed and lit another fag. I was tempted to say that smoking would be the death of her but as Maisie was a skeleton that would have been a pretty stupid remark.

The doorway that led from her office was rather low. As I was about to go through, I heard Maisie's raucous voice.

"Mind your head!" (Very funny.)

So I trooped up the stairs to see my boss. That's not strictly true because, as my boss was the Invisible Man, it wasn't possible to *see* him.

I entered cautiously as I knew the Invisible Man had a wicked sense of humour and liked to play tricks on people. He would stand by the door and stick his leg out so you tripped over it or, if he was in his *Boston Strangler* mood, creep up behind you and put his hands tightly round your throat, though that wouldn't worry me.

"Sit down," came a voice from behind the desk.

"You've been the *Horseman* for how long?"

"173 years," I replied.

"Time you had a change."

There was the sound of the Invisible Man getting up from his chair and of footsteps. A cupboard door seemed to open of its own accord and a head moved from a shelf in the cupboard, flew through the air - and landed on the desk in front of me.

"Recognise this?"

I certainly did.

"No, please," I begged. "Not Charles the First. Anyone but him."

"Don't worry," said my boss, soothingly. "You did Charles for nearly two centuries. That's enough for anyone. I have something completely new for you. These days, even we ghosts are under instructions to *modernise*."

He explained what the task was.

After he had finished, I had a question. "When do I start?"

"I'm surprised a man of your experience has to ask. When do you think you start?"

I was assigned the *Badbury Rings* beat for my first patrol. So that is where I am on the night of 31st October. Wind gusting eerily; moon peering through scudding clouds. Ideal haunting weather. Patiently I wait for my first victim.

Yes, this looks like it – no-one else in sight. Good. Let's go. Wow, this is quick. I've never travelled at such a speed. I'm closing fast. Small car. Driver only, male, middle aged. Perfect. Yes, he's seen me. His hair is standing on end; eyes wide with fright; mouth gaping open. He's lost control. The car swerves and crashes into the trees with a satisfying bang.

I punch the air in delight and shout "Yes!"

The Invisible Man was right. The age of the *Headless Horseman* is over. The age of the *Headless Hell's Angel* has begun.

The Door

                Sound of knocking

ARTICHOKE   Come in.
BRANSGORE   I can't. The door's locked.
ARTICHOKE   No it isn't.
BRANSGORE   It certainly is.
ARTICHOKE   The door isn't locked. You only think the door's locked.
BRANSGORE   What rubbish, I'm pulling the handle with all my strength.
ARTICHOKE   I know you are. Careful you don't break it.
BRANSGORE   If you won't unlock the door, slide the key under so that I can unlock it from my side.
ARTICHOKE   I keep telling you the door isn't locked. It's all in your mind. Anyway, I haven't got a key. Now, just calm down.
BRANSGORE   Calm down?
ARTICHOKE   Yes. And take a few deep breaths. *(pause)* That's better. Try now.

                Door opens

ARTICHOKE   I told you the door wasn't locked.
BRANSGORE   Where are you? I can't see you.
ARTICHOKE   That's because I might not be here.
BRANSGORE   What do you mean?
ARTICHOKE   I might not exist. I might be an apparition. No, not an apparition because then you *would* be able to see me. A sort of sonic ghost, perhaps. An audio phantom. Then again, I might be a figment of your imagination or –
BRANSGORE   Or what?
ARTICHOKE   Or I might be hiding in the wardrobe.

    BRANSGORE goes up to the wardrobe and tries the door
BRANSGORE   The wardrobe door is locked.
ARTICHOKE   No it isn't.
BRANSGORE   I'm not going to go through all that again. I've had enough of your games. I'm leaving.
ARTICHOKE   That's up to you. But, if you leave, you will never know.
BRANSGORE   What won't I know?
ARTICHOKE   Whether I'm hiding in the wardrobe or not.
BRANSGORE   No, I won't. And I don't care.
ARTICHOKE   Very well then. Goodbye.
BRANSGORE   Bloody good riddance, more like.
    A pause of several seconds
ARTICHOKE   I thought you were leaving the room.
BRANSGORE   I was. But I can't.
ARTICHOKE   Why can't you?
BRANSGORE   The door's locked.

Picture This

I picked up the local paper and a dramatic photograph caught my eye. Crop circles! They were still at it then. My mind went back thirty years and I was no longer a middle-aged man enjoying a leisurely weekend breakfast but a teenager standing on the edge of a moonlit Hampshire wheat field. Andy, my best friend, and I had just finished our A-levels and, depending upon the results, were hoping to go to University. We knew that financial stringency would soon force us to get summer jobs but it was still early July and we were enjoying the fine weather. Lack of money meant we had to create our own entertainment and one of the things we had found to keep us amused was making crop circles. We lived in a small town surrounded by rolling wheat fields. Who wouldn't be tempted? We had made three already that year and on the night in question had almost completed our fourth. We were staring at our handiwork when a voice behind us almost made us jump out of our skins.

"Not bad. Not bad at all and I consider myself rather an expert." It was an upper-class drawling voice though it did seem to have a rather metallic inhuman quality.

I turned round to face the speaker. He was a tall man, clad in a white overall. He was thin, very thin – like a stick insect. But it wasn't the man's extreme leanness that was the most remarkable feature; it was his head, which was entirely bald, skull-like and bright green. His eyes were almond-shaped and black, completely black with no iris or pupil or even eye-lashes. His mouth was a dark oblong, with no sign of lips or teeth.

I was still staring in amazement when I noticed something out of the corner of my eye. Standing in the field, next to our crop circle, was an object. It resembled two giant soup dishes, with the top one placed upside down on the lower one. The structure was about three metres high and six metres in diameter. From the lower soup dish, four spindly metallic legs protruded.

"I didn't see you land," I stammered.

"If we have the technology to voyage from our star system on the edge of the Galaxy don't you think we have the technology to remain invisible if we choose? You Earth people expect to see a flying saucer so a flying saucer is what you will see. Now you look like an adventurous couple of lads. Do you fancy coming for a spin?"

"Yes," said Andy.

"Yes," I said about three seconds later.

The thin man turned towards Andy.

"You spoke first."

What happened next was not like the movies. Red X-rays didn't emanate from the man's eyes and zap Andy. He wasn't surrounded by a translucent white glow, green slime didn't issue from his mouth and ears. He simply aged very, very, quickly. The long-haired eighteen year-old became a rather trendily-dressed twenty something, then a suited executive, next a substantial figure wearing some kind of chain of office. Soon he started to stoop, put on weight and his hair became grey. Finally, my best mate had been transformed into an old tramp, a scruffy derelict wearing a long overcoat. The whole process had taken no more than a minute.

"Do you still want to come?" asked the thin man.

"Yus," replied the vagrant and taking a swig of Cyprus sherry from a bottle which he carefully placed in a pocket of his greatcoat, he tottered towards the spaceship, climbing the ladder with some difficulty.

"We would never have taken you," the thin man said to me. "You are young with your whole life before you. It wouldn't have been fair. I misinformed you, I'm afraid. We are not going for a 'spin'. That disgusting tramp is coming back with us – just as well we have no sense of smell. Revolting creature that he is, there is within his bloated and diseased carcase all the material we need to manufacture a 'clone'. No disrespect, old chap, but I hope we are never sufficiently desperate to need to invade your primitive and well, rather barbaric planet. But if we ever do, we will be able to create a limitless supply of 'native inhabitants' to replace the indigenous population which we will, of course, have to vaporise. Besides, our astro-biologists have been wanting to get their hands on an Earthling for ages. They can't understand how evolution, normally such a benign and positive process, has managed to produce such a malevolent mutation as the human race."

"You say you won't take me because I'm young. But you have taken Andy and he is the same age as me."

"We haven't taken Andy. We've taken that drunken old vagrant. You have just seen him climb aboard our flying saucer."

"B-but -" I stammered.

"Listen, old chap. I know you are rather down in the mouth. We'll put on a little display for you as we leave. By the way, do you have a camera with you?"

"Yes," I replied. In those days, I was a keen photographer and the Leica camera, which my parents had given me for my eighteenth birthday, was one of my prize possessions. I used to take the camera with me on our nocturnal expeditions because as well as making crop circles, Andy and I had a plan to manufacture some ghost photos which we naively hoped to sell to newspapers for a great deal of money. So far all our attempts had proved laughable failures.

"Better get weaving," said the thin man. "So long old boy." With that, he turned on his heels and climbed into the spaceship. The ladder retracted and the door closed. The thin man was as good as his word. He certainly did put on a little display. The saucer rose vertically about twenty feet or so and then made its way across the wheat field going at about thirty miles an hour. Red lights were flashing from the top and the bottom and from several places on the rim. All the while, the machine was emitting a loud bleeping sound. I had no idea whether my camera would be able to get any usable pictures but even if the odds were 1000/1, the rewards of obtaining a genuine flying saucer picture were so enormous in terms of both fame and fortune that I snapped away furiously.

The saucer carried on like that for half a mile or so, then the bleeping stopped and the lights were switched off. I lost sight of it in the gloom. I soon saw it again. This time the spaceship was flying very fast and very low and it was heading straight for me. I started to run but soon realised there was no point. I hit the ground and lay flat on my back, rigid with fear. I swear the saucer passed no more than six feet above my head. Then it rose vertically and began to spin violently with bright sparks showering from it like a manic Catherine wheel.

I quickly grabbed my camera and took a few more shots before the machine disappeared into the night sky. Of course I was concerned about Andy but really there was little I could do, so I went home and crept up to bed. I lay awake for an hour or two and then fell into a deep sleep.

The next thing I knew was Mum shouting, "Pete – phone." I

stumbled downstairs hardly awake. I checked my watch. Quarter past nine.

"Sorry, mate. About last night. I just crashed out. Too tired. All Janey's fault." Janey was Andy's girl-friend. Despite all his boasting I don't think he was actually screwing her. At least that is what Janey tells me and I believe her. I had better – I've been married to her for nearly twenty-five years.

The voice sounded like Andy but that wasn't enough for me. I needed to actually see him. "Do you fancy a coffee later? Courtyard Café 11.30. Okay?"

"Okay, mate. See ya."

When I arrived at the Courtyard there was Andy, sitting at a table, long hair, torn jeans, scruffy sweater – gazing moodily into his coffee. He looked up when I came in. I suppose I must have stood there staring at him.

"What's up, Pete, mate? You look as though you've seen a ghost."

"No, it's just, er," I stammered. I wanted to touch Andy to see if he was real. You didn't hug your male friends in those days.

"What did you do when I didn't turn up. Just waited around, I suppose. How long did you stay in the wheat field?"

"Oh, I dunno. About an hour and a half I guess."

"Sorry, mate, I reckon that must have been a really boring hour and a half."

"It certainly was," I replied.

As I said, I was a keen photographer. I had a makeshift darkroom in my parents' house. So later, I went to develop the film I had taken in the wheat field. I didn't hold out too much hope and I was right. My camera just wasn't good enough to produce any recognisable images, even in the moonlight. I was disappointed but not surprised.

About ten days later, an envelope, addressed to me, arrived from Kodak. This was unexpected. Though, as I've said, I normally developed my own films, I would sometimes send negatives away to be processed professionally but I hadn't posted anything to Kodak recently. I opened the envelope and literally gasped in astonishment. There were eight prints inside. Four showed the flying saucer doing its bleeping run across the field and four the machine in Catherine wheel mode. And they were of stunning clarity. I must have sat at the dining room table for several minutes staring at the pictures in wonderment – occasionally picking them up to examine them more closely.

"How disappointing for you. Are they all like that?" It was my mother's voice. She had crept up behind me and was looking over my shoulder. I had been too absorbed to hear her footsteps. On the table, face up, were three of the photos.

"I hope there's nothing wrong with the camera. I wonder why they are all that strange uniform grey colour. It's as if you laid on your back on a dull day, pointed the camera upwards and started photographing the cloud. Even you aren't daft enough to do that." Then she muttered under her breath. "Oh, I don't know, though."

What was the matter with my mother? Had she finally flipped or had her eyesight failed completely? The three pictures on the table quite clearly showed the spaceship on its 'bleeping' run across the field. Still, best to humour her.

"No Mum," I said. "The camera is fine. It was my fault." I gave her rather a curious look, put the prints back in their envelope and went up to my room.

My mother's comments had sowed a seed of doubt in my mind. I wouldn't phone the pictures editor of the *Daily Mirror* just yet. I was due to meet Andy later so I took two of the photographs with me and showed them to him.

"What do you make of these?"

"I dunno. You're supposed to be the expert. For some reason, they've come out all grey. What happened? Did light get in?"

Over the years, I have shown the pictures to several people. Usually, I will put a couple of them in amongst other photos, such as holiday snaps and the reaction has always been the same. Everyone, except me, sees them as a uniform grey colour.

I still have them. Prints fade over thirty years, particularly those taken by amateurs. But these are as bright and clear as when I first saw them. They are not even dog-eared, as they should be after the number of times I have handled them.

I have to be careful with my 'Flying Saucer' photographs, though. Once Janey was going to throw them away and was surprised when I wouldn't let her.

"Who wants to keep a load of old 'grey' pictures?" she asked incredulously.

I do.

The Watcher on the Shore

Though the watcher on the shore had been waiting in the moonlight for many nights, when he saw a figure move in the shadows he became instantly alert.

The woman, she was a young woman, walked serenely into the calm water. She continued with measured step as the sea came up to her ankles and then over her knees.

The watcher had to move fast but he had prepared most of his life for this moment and he was able to rescue the child the woman had been carrying in her arms. As for the woman – he wouldn't think of the woman.

The child, a boy child, grew into a man and, because that is how things are ordered he has now become the watcher on the shore. He knows that one night a woman will walk into the sea carrying a child and he will have to save that child as he was himself saved.

What he does not know is that the woman will fight fiercely. So fiercely that he will have to forget about the child and fight for his own life. Even when he has subdued the woman and can reach for the half-conscious child, she will continue to struggle and he will need to hold her head under water until she moves no more.

This is the test to which the watcher will be put, made more difficult because of his secret fear of drowning – occasioned perhaps by some half-forgotten distant memory.

The Unhappy Prince

"I hate to admit it, darling but Mummy was right, you *do* have to be born royal to make a success of the job. Poor dear! It's not your fault."

The prince agreed with his wife. That remark summed up the state of their marriage. Boredom. At forty, the princess was tall, elegant and, well, regal – but she seemed to have little enthusiasm for anything. Certainly not for her husband.

How different from that glorious summer day all those years ago when the giggling teenage girl had picked him up, given him a big sloppy kiss and turned him from an ugly frog into a handsome prince.

At first, everything had been perfect. The young couple had a grand, almost fairy-tale, wedding. Life in the palace with smart clothes, soft beds, ornate furniture, exquisite food, musicians and poets to entertain them had been a wonderful contrast to his previous cold, monotonous, miserable aquatic existence. And they *were* so much in love.

Yet the Prince felt he never fitted in. He knew the servile courtiers, so friendly to his face, were sniggering behind his back. His wife, now so indifferent to him, might have taken a lover from amongst the toffee-nosed chinless wonders who comprised what passed for an aristocracy, or maybe not. He couldn't tell.

Maybe he was not quite the Prince Charming of twenty years ago; true he had put on a little weight and his hair was thinning, but he was still a good-looking man. He was sure though that if *he* ever bedded a serving wench, *she* would be certain to find out.

Their two children, a boy and a girl, who had looked so angelic in the royal nursery, were now argumentative, stroppy teenagers with little respect for a dad who had once been a tadpole.

Recently, there had been growing unrest in the kingdom. A series of poor harvests had led to a food shortage and a few months ago an angry mob had gathered at the palace gates.

"Can't you do something, darling?" asked the princess, as though it was his fault there was no bread. What was he supposed to do? He wasn't a baker. Anyway, he had no sympathy for the peasants. If they had no bread, they could always eat cake.

One autumn afternoon, the prince was strolling gloomily in the gardens when his steps took him towards his old home, the frog pond. He recognised the special stone easily enough. He picked it up and stroked it.

"Wot do you want?" a raucous cockney voice asked. There, in front of him, suspended in mid-air was the genie, just as he remembered her – two feet tall and wearing a white dress. She had golden hair, blue eyes and a dazzling smile. He had forgotten about the corncrake voice.

"I...er...want to be turned back into a frog."

"*Wot!*" shrieked the genie. "You ungrateful bastard. You want to give up life as a prince?"

"Er...yes."

"After everything I've done for you!" yelled the genie. She was really getting into her stride. The prince should have known that Hell hath no fury like a genie scorned. "Of all the hundreds of frogs I could have got the princess to kiss, I chose you. I put you in her hand. I cast my spell and transformed you into a handsome prince. And now you want to go back to being a frog?"

"Yes."

"Go on then."

"Go on what?" asked the prince.

"Turn back into a frog."

"Aren't you going to wave your magic wand and say some special words?"

"Give me strength," screeched the genie. "What do you think this is, a bleeding pantomime? No I am not going to wave my wand and say some magic words. Please yourself. Turn back into a frog or not. I couldn't care less. I'm off."

With that remark the genie disappeared. When the Prince

looked down, he saw that he was squatting on a rock in the middle of the pond. He had been granted his wish. The one-time prince found his froggy friends more genuine than the fawning palace flunkies and life as an amphibian was far less stressful than life as a member of the royal family.

It is said that, in the following year, there was a violent revolution, that the palace was destroyed and the inhabitants done to death in various gruesome ways. Safe in his pond the frog (who had once been a prince) neither knew nor cared.

The Boat

"Dad's still out there, then."

"Yes, he never stops. Morning, noon and night."

The speakers were mother and son. How old were they? Well, ages are a little bit tricky in this account. Let us just say that the son was grown-up and the mother didn't appear to be elderly.

"Is it the same old story? Does he say he's been talking to God again?" asked the son.

"Perhaps, Shem, he *has* been talking to God. Maybe God did tell him to build a boat."

"Maybe. But why can't he be like other old guys with time on their hands and make a model yacht for his grandchildren to sail in the pond, or construct a *ship in a bottle?*"

"You know your dad, how stubborn he is. He'll never give up," said the mother scornfully. "He'll keep on working until he drops, even though he won't finish that boat if he lives to be a thousand."

Outside, an old man was hammering away in the broiling heat. There hadn't been any rain for months; the area was enduring the longest drought anybody could remember, which made the boat he was working on look even more incongruous than it would in a rainy country, though it was certainly an impressive sight, towering over the neighbourhood. People would stop and stare. Most would just shake their heads and mutter, "That guy's crazy." But there were three young tearaways who were notorious in the town as they were always on the lookout to cause trouble. They found the old boat-builder an inviting target for their sarcastic wit.

"Hey, look at that," said one. "The thing is almost finished. He will soon be able to launch it."

"How can the silly old fucker launch it?" asked another. "We are miles from the sea."

"Don't mock," warned the third. "God told him to build it." He looked up and shouted, "Isn't that so?"

"Yes it is, you young blasphemer," replied the old man.

"But why would God ask anyone to build a boat?" queried the first tearaway. "God doesn't need boats. If He wants to cross a lake, or even an ocean, He can just walk on top of the water. Doesn't even get His feet wet."

"Perhaps God will create a new sea 'specially for this boat to float on," said one of his mates.

The old man shook his fist in anger at the hooligans. He shook it so vigorously that he dropped his hammer. One of the lads picked it up and all three ran away laughing.

Eventually though, despite all the negative comments, the boat *was* finished. The old man called all his family together – his wife, his three sons, their wives and children.

"I am pleased to say that my task is completed. You might wonder why I have spent so much time on it."

"Because you are a senile old fool," muttered one of the sons under his breath.

"I heard that. I'm not as deaf as you think. The boat was built for a purpose."

"God's purpose?" asked another son.

"Yes, God's purpose."

"Are we going on a voyage in your boat?" said an 8 year-old (female) grandchild. (We don't have a problem with kids. It's when we get to adults, particularly very old adults, that the method of age numbering becomes shall we say 'complicated'.)

The girl looked round at the assembled family members. "But there are only fifteen of us altogether and the boat is enormous. We won't need all that space."

"Miriam is right," agreed her 11 year-old brother. "The boat is fucking enormous."

"Wash your mouth out, Reuben," ordered the boy's mother. "How many times have I told you not to use that word?"

"What, 'enormous'? But it *is* fucking enormous."

"Seeing as you seem to have all the answers, dear father, tell me this," said the son who had muttered 'senile old fool'. "How are we going to get the boat anywhere near a lake or sea? How are we going to launch it?"

"We are not going to launch it. We don't have to. We are simply going to go inside that's all."

"And wait for a miracle, I suppose?"

"Something like that," replied the old man.

"Oh for Christ's sake, talk sense."

"You can't say 'for Christ's sake'," piped up Reuben. "That's an anachronism. Christ won't be born for another thousand years."

"Clever little bastard, aren't you? Oh very well. For Jehovah's sake talk sense."

"Always you Shem, isn't it?" said the old man. "Always the one to argue."

Shem was in no mood to be silenced. "Just because you are head of the family and think you have a direct line to God that doesn't mean we are all going to clamber into this enormous boat, situated miles from the sea and sit around waiting for a miracle."

"There won't only be us."

"Don't tell me you have invited the neighbours as well?"

"Not exactly."

Strange sounds could be heard coming from outside – animal noises. There were grunts, barks, miaows, brays, snorts, bleats and howls. Shem opened the door and peered out. The backyard was crammed full of creatures of all kinds. He could see pigs, dogs, goats, donkeys, sheep, cows, cats, wolves and, judging by the racket he was hearing, there must have been other animals which were out of sight.

"Holy Moses," he exclaimed. Reuben shook his head.

Shem tried again. "I just don't Adam and Eve it." Reuben gave the thumbs up sign.

The old man went out into the yard and held up his hands. "Quiet you lot." Surprisingly the animals fell silent. "Now line up in order. You know what to do. We have practised this often enough."

To Shem's amazement, the animals began to form up into a long line. It was then he realised that there were 2 of each species. 2 cats, 2 dogs, 2 donkeys, 2 sheep, 2 pigs and so on.

"Right," said the old man. "Time to come on board. Keep in your pairs please. I want no shoving, no pushing, no queue jumping. Wait your turn. There is plenty of room for everyone."

Then, like an exceptionally well-behaved class on a school outing, the animals filed onto the boat, 2 by 2.

Once the animals were settled, it was time for the family to board. As they were doing so Shem jostled against a young woman aged about twenty whom he didn't recognise. At least, he thought she was a woman but she was dressed more like a boy and had short hair, close-cropped.

"Excuse me, you aren't one of us," he said. "You have no right to get on to this boat."

"I have every right," she replied in an extremely dodgy French accent.

Shem wasn't convinced. He shook his head.

"But I really do. You see, my name is Joan. I am Joan of the Ark."

For seven days, nothing happened. With the animals aboard, it was humid, stuffy and very noisy on the Ark but Noah's authority was absolute. Despite Shem's constant moaning, he had no intention of leaving. He really did believe that his father was in contact with the Almighty and he knew that 'The Lord thy God is a jealous God' and could not be disobeyed without serious consequences. You might think it foolish of him then to attempt to seduce Joan in view of the clear prohibition 'Thou Shalt Not Commit Adultery'. But it must be remembered that the Ten Commandments had not yet been issued. He didn't have any success with Joan, who was extremely virtuous and spent more time praying than any of them. "She must be a lesbian," Shem muttered sourly.

The weather became hotter with the sun burning down from a clear blue sky. On the afternoon of the seventh day, however, the clouds rolled in – immense, steepling, sinister, thunder clouds. The sky darkened and the rain began. And what rain. Huge drops crashed against the planks of the Ark but Noah had built his boat well and it withstood the storm. Several times, Shem peered out of the window but all he could see was an unrelenting curtain of rain.

They settled down for the night because, as Noah said, "It is far too dangerous for anyone to go up on deck in this weather." Shortly before dawn, Shem woke with a start. The rain was still hammering down relentlessly but he felt the boat judder. Then he heard a sort of scraping sound and, a few minutes later, the Ark definitely moved. They were floating. Shem thought of waking his father who was sleeping peacefully but decided not to. The old man had never doubted, never wavered in his faith.

The rain continued falling heavily for a week before it eased off somewhat. The skies were a leaden grey and the cessation of the downpour proved to be only a brief respite in the deluge. Nevertheless, it was possible to get up on deck and survey the scene. Noah and his family lived in a flat country with hardly any high ground.

The whole area was completely flooded and the waters stretched as far as the eye could see. However, there was one hill, though a small hill, in the district and on top of this hill was a tall cedar tree, the uppermost branches of which were poking above the flood. Clinging to these branches were three figures. As the boat drifted nearer, Noah recognised that these were the youths who had continuously tormented him while he was building the Ark.

They shouted and waved when they saw the boat. Eager to grasp at any chance of survival, they dived into the flood and started to swim towards it. Just then a breeze sprang up and took the Ark further away from the cedar tree.

The boys began to struggle and first one sank beneath the waves and then another. The Ark was still being blown by the wind and it was clear that the third hooligan was not going to make it, either.

All this put Noah in an excellent mood. He reached for his acoustic guitar. He had gained quite a reputation around the folk clubs when he was younger, but with most of his time taken up with building the Ark, he hadn't played much recently. He strummed a few chords and shook his head. Then he smiled. "Oh yes," he whispered. "This is the one."

> *"Come gather round people wherever you roam*
> *And admit that the waters around you have grown*
> *Accept it that soon you'll be drenched to the bone*
> *You better start swimmin' or you'll sink like a stone."*

Noah then stopped playing and chuckled to himself.

"Gee, I must really be getting old. I can't remember the next line."

No direction home. A confused bear at the North Pole.

Burglar Bill's Nasty Experience.

"I tell you there is a fortune in that place – medals, statues, cups and it's all solid silver." The speaker was a gangly, pimply youth of about 18, with long, rather greasy hair, wearing a leather jacket, dirty jeans and a Sid Vicious T-shirt. "My nan cleans for that Major Patterson, so I know what I'm talking about. He was a crack shot in the army and played polo for England. That's why there's so many trophies. No alarms, he doesn't believe in them." He assumed a posh accent. *"I'm an old soldier, don't you know and I can deal with any intruders."*

A small, neat middle-aged man wearing a dark raincoat sat quietly in the corner of the *Three Feathers,* sipping a pint of bitter. He had short-cropped grey hair and watchful eyes. He didn't appear to be paying any attention to what the boastful lad was saying but he heard and remembered every word. He knew all about Terry Mackenzie. Mugging pensioners, or bursting into some old lady's flat and nicking her rent money was his kind of work.

Terry was probably right concerning the valuable trophies the major kept in his house but it was all swagger – Terry lacked the nerve or skill to attempt a job like that and wouldn't do anything about it, but others might. "Yes," thought Bill Townsend. "Others might."

A few days later, the quiet man in the pub was strolling along Acacia Avenue – to all intents and purposes just an ordinary law abiding citizen enjoying a leisurely stroll down a leafy suburban road. Nobody would notice him paying particular attention to number 42, which was where Major Patterson lived, but he was surreptitiously taking in the details of the gate, the fence, the drive, the number and position of the windows – and a thousand other details which a man of his capabilities could memorise in an instant. In any case it *was* a fine spring day and although this was work rather than pleasure, Bill Townsend *was* enjoying his afternoon walk.

A week after that, Bill climbed through a downstairs window of number 42. It was 2 am and he didn't want to disturb the owner by ringing the door bell. Bill then took off his coat. Though good at his job he didn't like being watched doing it. Neither did he like people to know *where* he was working so he wore dark clothes on the way to work, trying to be as inconspicuous as possible and, for the same reason, he usually worked at night.

However Bill was a traditionalist and never felt happy going about his nefarious business unless he was clad in the time-honoured yellow and black striped burglar's jersey. He took a folded super strong plastic bin-liner from his pocket. (One had to move with the times.) In the darkness, it wasn't possible to see the word 'SWAG' emblazoned on the side, but Bill knew it was there and that made him feel more comfortable.

Bill soon got his bearings. This was the lounge, so the study must be to the left. His torch-beam swept round the room and lit up a dark shape in front of the gas-fire. Bill edged closer and saw that the shape had a head, a tail and paws. A DOG! But fast asleep. Bill waited a moment or two. The shape didn't stir. Decision time. Should he beat a retreat? *NO, GO FOR IT.*

Cautiously, Bill moved towards the study. There was the desk, the window, the armchair and then a glint of silver in his torch beam. Yes, the trophy cabinet. At a glance, Bill could see that the little rat had been right. It was full of cups, statuettes and medals. Bill eased the cabinet open and filled his swag-bag, then crept back into the lounge. Perhaps he was getting a little old for this job because his left foot caught a table leg and sent him flying. The swag-bag hit the ground with a tremendous crash. Bill hit the ground with a dull thud and a moan.

"*Jesus, the dog!*" was Bill's first thought, as he lay on the carpet in pain, clutching his knee. But the dog never stirred, still sleeping peacefully. The house returned to quietness and Bill was beginning to think that he was safe as he got gingerly to his feet and started to pick up his ill-gotten gains.

Suddenly, there was a loud thumping sound of heavy footsteps, a door was flung open and the room was flooded with light. Bill stood rooted to the spot, blinking at the sudden brightness. An elderly man, with white hair, a military moustache and bloodshot eyes appeared in the doorway. He bared his yellowing teeth and launched himself at Bill.

"Woof, woof, woof." Bill, confused, turned towards the fireplace, afraid that the dog had woken at last. Then, to his surprise, he realised that the noises had come not from the dog, which was still fast asleep, but the man.

Bill backed away, still hobbling.

"Woof, woof," went Major Patterson and launched himself at Bill. His teeth caught Bill on the arm and ripped the sleeve of his striped jersey. Sheer panic gave Bill surprising energy. He raced over to the window, opened it and dived headlong through. He landed badly, grazing his hands and bruising his shoulder. He picked himself up and ran across the lawn as fast as his aging (and injured) legs would carry him.

Bill didn't stop until he reached the road, then he looked anxiously behind him. He hadn't been followed, but he could hear the sound. "Woof, woof, woof."

Bill was out of breath, and his hands, shoulder and knee hurt like hell. What a night! Just like him to break into the house of a man who kept a dog and barked himself.

Climate change. Baked Alaska.

Eeyore's Cathedral

One fine day, Pooh and Piglet found Eeyore in a corner of his field standing beside what looked like a heap of sticks but, knowing Eeyore, was probably his new home.

"Hello, Eeyore," said Pooh. "I see you have got a new home."

"It's not a new home, it's my cathedral."

"What's a cathedral?" asked Piglet.

"A cathedral," replied Eeyore, with great dignity, "is where I worship. Donkeys may be lowly creatures but they ought to worship their Maker, even though He made them on one of his, shall we say, made them on one of his more clumsy days."

That night, there was a fierce storm. Everyone was frightened. Pooh burrowed beneath the covers, Piglet hid under the bed and even Tigger lost his bounce.

Next morning, Pooh and Piglet went to visit Eeyore. There was no sign of his cathedral, just a lot of sticks scattered all over the field.

"Were you afraid of the storm?" asked Pooh.

"No," replied Eeyore.

"Neither was I," boasted Pooh. "I wish the storm had happened in the daytime then I would have gone up with my balloon to take a better look."

"Never mind that," said Eeyore. "My cathedral has blown down and I have to stand outside in the wind and rain. I can't worship my Maker any more."

"Can't you worship your Maker while standing outside in the wind and rain?" asked Piglet.

Eeyore thought for a long time. He wasn't sure if he *could* worship his Maker while standing outside in the wind and rain. But he could try.

Dr Gilchrist's Eventful Morning

On a fine sunny morning in the late seventeenth century, Dr Walter Gilchrist, self-proclaimed eminent mathematician, philosopher, naturalist and astronomer was walking along New College Street lost in thought – he was using his great brain to consider how many angels could gavotte on the head of a pin and was totally oblivious of his surroundings. Just then, his right foot slipped on a pile of excrement. Dr Gilchrist stumbled, almost fell, then cursed. Shit was clearly no respecter of academic reputations. As he scraped the mess from his shoe, he saw, out of the corner of his eye, an object falling from a nearby tenement. A speck at first, it became larger and Dr Gilchrist thought that it was a small parcel but then the object grew arms and legs and he realised that it was a baby.

In his youth, Dr Gilchrist had been a noted exponent of the Edinburgh Medicineball Game which, for those who don't know, is rather like a cross between a rugby match played by psychopaths and a 20 man-a-side cage fight. Despite being well-advanced into portly middle-age, Dr Gilchrist took a couple of steps forward and neatly caught the baby, which was entirely naked. The good doctor was so engrossed that he scarcely noticed a shower of warm soapy water which drenched him soon after he caught the baby.

With his huge brain and its extensive knowledge of dynamics, ballistics and meteorology, Dr Gilchrist was easily able to identify the window through which the baby must have left the building. "Sixth floor third from left," he said to himself.

Carrying the baby, Dr Gilchrist entered the tenement and by the time he had reached the sixth floor was puffing somewhat. He paused for a moment to regain his breath. Of course, he had retained an image of the layout of the building in his great mind, so he was able to calculate which apartment the baby had come from.

He knocked on the appropriate door.

It was answered by a shuffling, slovenly woman wearing a grubby maid's uniform. She had dark hair, a pale face, buck teeth and looked at Dr Gilchrist with a moronic stare.

"Good morning. Is this yours?"

The woman didn't reply, just wiped the snot from her runny nose with her filthy sleeve.

Then an elegantly-clad middle-aged lady appeared from the other side of the room.

"What is it, Marie?" she asked.

Marie continued to gawp sullenly. Dr Gilchrist edged past her and spoke to the elegant lady.

"Good morning, madam. Does he belong to you?"

Dr Gilchrist gave the baby to the lady who took him in her arms and turned him over, inspecting him carefully, as though he was an expensive piece of china she was considering buying.

"He might. I will go and check." She went out of the room for a few minutes, then returned – without the baby.

"He *could* be Robbie," she said doubtfully. "Anyway, the crib was empty, so I've put him in it. At least if he isn't Robbie, he will keep it warm for him."

Dr Gilchrist touched his hat, bade the ladies "Good day" and walked out of the apartment, closing the door behind him. As he did so, he heard the voice of the elegant lady. "How many times must I tell you, Marie? *Don't throw the baby out with the bathwater.*"

Dr Gilchrist descended the stairs and resumed his stroll towards the university. It is to be hoped that in the half-hour or so that it took him to get there, no more infants were ejected from windows in New College Street. The good doctor was so preoccupied in mentally solving an exciting quadratic equation that he wouldn't even have noticed any falling children, let alone caught them, unless one had landed on his head – which did not in fact happen.

Eurostar Adventure

I pay off the cab outside St Pancras with a slightly-damp newly-printed £20 note. I head for the gents, wash my inky fingers and it strikes me that St Pancras isn't really a railway station at all – more like a cross between a shopping mall and a recently-refurbished regional airport.

How very different from the grimy Paddington of my childhood. Then you could *smell* the smoke, *feel* the steam on your face, *hear* the *puff-puff-puff* as the train pulled away. I remember the distinctive odour of city soot that clung to my clothes after a visit to London.

Today, I'm going to Paris on Eurostar – alone. My original travelling companion, Rebecca, cancelled, claiming she was attacked by a flock of birds. Just as well, really, Rebecca has no head for heights and would surely have suffered from vertigo if we had gone up the Eiffel Tower. I then tried to call Marion to offer her the ticket but she couldn't come to the phone as she was taking a shower.

When I get to the check in, I see a notice: *Prohibited Objects* – a list of items you aren't allowed to take on the train. Included in the list are guns. Damn, I was going to wait until we were halfway through the Tunnel, stand up and shout *Your money or your life,* relieve the passengers of their valuables, stuff all the loot into my *Louis Vuitton* attaché case, pull the euro-equivalent of the communication cord, then make off into the darkness, firing wildly to discourage my pursuers.

I'm basically law-abiding, so I drop my Colt 45 into the recycling bin.

As I am about to board Eurostar, I spy, further along the platform, a rotund figure wearing a dark overcoat, trilby hat and sporting a ludicrous waxed moustache. *HERCULE POIROT.* That changes everything. Now I'm determined to commit murder AND get away with it - I need to prove that my *little grey cells* are superior to his and publicly humiliate him. Just think of it. *Poirot Fucks Up.* A guaranteed best seller but it would finish him off for good. I take my seat and try to formulate a plan. I have the answer. I WILL KILL SOMEONE I DON'T KNOW. Perfect. *Strangers on a Train.* After I have committed the murder I will make my escape by means of Patricia Highsmith's typewriter and become a character in a completely different novel while the narcissistic Belgian gumshoe is still enmeshed in his unreadable Agatha Christie crap. How will I commit murder now I've thrown away my gun? I don't know. Strangle someone with my shoelace if necessary – but I MUST get the better of Poirot.

I had better make a start, I don't want Tom Ripley to beat me to it. I set off down the train looking for a victim, chosen by random. I receive a surprise as I step into the next carriage. No longer am I faced with the airline-style seating of Eurostar – I'm in a long corridor, with a series of wooden doors on one side. This is an old-fashioned sleeping-car.

Outside one of the compartments, there is a line of about a dozen people, dressed in 1930s style. These people enter the compartment one-by-one, remain in there for a minute or so, then leave. As each person emerges, they have a smile of satisfaction on their face. Then I notice that every one of them is carrying some lethal weapon: a sweet-looking old lady has a smoking gun, a pale youth brandishes a silver candlestick, a deferential butler is clutching a piece of lead piping and the wagon-lit attendant is thoughtfully replacing the cap on a bottle labelled *poison*.

Yes, I'm on the *Orient Express*. So what, I like to travel in outdated luxury. But then to my horror, I realise that I'm holding a gory dagger in my hand and drops of bright red blood are falling onto the plush carpet.

I look up and there stands Poirot. There is a disgusting smirk of triumph on his egg-shaped face.

"Bonsoir, mon ami. As they say, I 'ave you 'bang to rights'."

That's it, I'm trapped. I can hardly expect to leap out of a speeding train into the night and survive. I'm not James Bond.

I have only one chance. I reach inside my jacket pocket and pull out a slimy and foul-smelling fish. I fling the fish in the air so it passes over Poirot and lands with a splat on the floor behind him. He doesn't even turn his head; a detective of Poirot's calibre isn't going to be distracted by a red herring.

I turn to flee although I have no idea of where I hope to run to. Then I see a tall, rather-overweight, middle-aged gentleman with a pudgy face, wearing a grey-flannel suit and stetson hat.

"Please help me, sir. I'm an innocent man," I cry in anguish.

"Don't you know I'm retired?" the gentleman replies in an American accent.

"Couldn't you write just one more novel?"

"Okay, I'll do it." I go up to the man and give him a hug of gratitude. Forgetting that I am still holding the dagger, I almost accidentally stab Erle Stanley Gardner in the back. But I know I'm safe. I am certain to be found not guilty now that I've got Perry Mason to defend me.

An Unforeseen Delay.

A funeral procession was winding slowly towards the door of a country church on a slate-grey November afternoon with a numbing chill in the air which seeped into your very bones. At the front was the undertaker, then six pall bearers carrying the coffin followed by a shivering gaggle of relatives and friends.

"Nice day for it," said a fat, jolly man to a pale young woman.

"He was my stepfather," she wailed and burst into tears.

"All right, keep your hair on. I was only trying to be friendly."

As the procession neared the church door, it slowed even more then shuffled to a complete halt. Most people stood around in embarrassed silence, unaware of the correct etiquette for such an occasion. Not the fat, jolly man though.

"Good for business, eh?" he said and nudged the funeral director in the ribs. "If we have to stand around in the cold for much longer, I reckon a few of the old 'uns here will soon be in need of your services. And I read in the paper that there's a 'flu epidemic on the way. You must be coining it, mate."

The undertaker ignored him but glanced anxiously at his watch. He was facing a difficult dilemma. It was well past the scheduled starting time but, in these circumstances they could hardly begin the proceedings – could they?

Just then, one of the mourners shouted, "There he is."

Running up the lane with giant strides came a gaunt figure, deathly pale, wearing a top hat and a dark suit that had seen better days. This strange being vaulted the cemetery wall as though he were an Olympic athlete and then with one enormous bound, leapt into the coffin. As the watching crowd clapped and cheered, he removed his top hat, lay flat on his back and slammed down the coffin lid – the man who was late for his own funeral.

The Writer

He was in his mid-fifties dressed in jeans and a check shirt. He was so engrossed in his work that sunny morning that I was able to walk up close behind without him noticing. On a bench was a piece of board about six feet by three on which was traced in pencil outline the words 'Roy Anderson, Electrical Contractor' together with a telephone number. He was meticulously painting in the 'O' of 'Anderson'. Then he stood up and grimaced.

"Not good for the back, this work. That's a new sign for Roy's van."

"You are certainly doing a careful job."

"I've been doing this for over thirty years. Mind you, I'm not completely self-taught. I was one of the first students at the Creative Writing Course at the University of West Anglia run by Malcolm Cabbage in the 1980s. I was actually back at UWA only last year attending a class reunion. There had been twenty three of us and just fourteen made the reunion. The place had changed a lot, the campus was crammed with huge buildings made of concrete and glass whereas our classes had been held in Farmer Bryson's barn. We students sat on bales of hay with a pile of rotting mangelwurzels at the back.

We old timers received a very friendly reception and were invited to visit a Flash Fiction Workshop. There were about forty students, all sitting at computers. The tutor typed a word which was shown on a big screen. Then every student typed the same word. The tutor typed another word which also flashed up on the screen and the students typed that and so it went on, all forty students typing in unison. In less than ten minutes they had finished. Each student had produced an absolutely identical story of exactly 200 words. I was most impressed.

The poetry group was very different. The students were still sitting behind computers, of course, not a pen or piece of paper in sight, but there were only about fifteen of them. Each person typed a line of poetry on their computer, then moved round one place and typed a line of poetry on that computer, then moved round one place again and typed another line. This process continued until the tutor shouted, "Stop." Whatever you had in front of you at that moment became 'your' poem. It might seem to be rather a random way of working but Sylvia Ayres-Duffy won the Andrew Doggerel Cup with her poem written using this method. She didn't get the prize for best collection, though – that went to the one-armed bloke who sits on the pavement all day outside Sainsbury's rattling his tin.

The Most Unreadable Novel award went to 'Bride and Brejudice' by Kevin Cement-Mixer (who is perhaps better-known as a concrete poet). This caused some controversy as it was alleged that Cement-Mixer's novel bore a remarkable similarity to a book by an obscure nineteenth century spinster. But who reads Jane Morris nowadays? Anyway as far as the academic world is concerned, the concept of plagiarism is now totally outdated. Cement-Mixer had certainly put in a lot of work. He went through the entire novel substituting the letter 'B' for the letter 'P'. Then had to start again and insert the word 'fuck' eighteen times in every paragraph. Yes, I believe Kevin Cement-Mixer deserved his prize for effort alone.

As I mentioned, the present staff were very friendly to us former students except when somebody muttered the words 'degree factory'. Then the atmosphere turned decidedly frosty. But I can't stand here chatting all day."

The writer then started to paint in the final 'n' of 'Anderson'.

"You know something. As I said, there were fourteen of us at the reunion and we have all followed different careers. Three, at least became TV producers and three more went into advertising. Carol Smythe is a tree surgeon, Ken Fothergill a Labour MP and Tom Robinson is a deckhand on the Isle of Wight ferry. But of the fourteen of us who were on that 'Creative Writing' course all those years ago, I'm the only one still making his living by writing."

Bruce Springsteen's Autobiography

I went up on stage
I played my guitar
I sang some songs
I did this for 50 years

THE END

If you enjoyed this book, please recommend it to your friends.
If you didn't, please recommend it to your enemies.